canning circus

For Margaret,

thanks so much for coming,

Christopher Prosser

canning circus

a novel under and over nottingham

christopher pressler

Heartland Publishing

First published in 2001 by Heartland Publishing Limited
P.O. Box 902, Sutton Valence, Maidstone, Kent ME17 3HY

ISBN 0 9525187 2 4

British Library Cataloguing-In-Publication data

A catalogue record for this book is available
from the British Library.

Typeset in Bodoni 10/13.5 pt
Book design by Jeff Horne

Front cover photograph by Christopher Pressler
Back cover photograph by Ross Clark
Chapter heading photographs by John Spiers

Printed and bound in Great Britain
on acid-free paper from sustainable forests
by Antony Rowe Ltd., Chippenham.

to G.B.
for Sherwood days

How shall we find the concord of this discord?

William Shakespeare

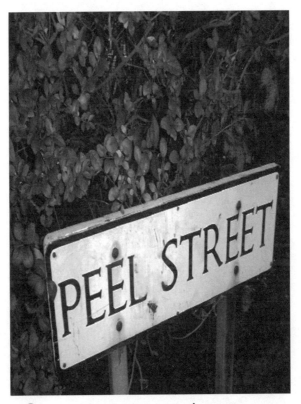

chapter **1** tigguacobaucc

a person and a place

T HIS is the greatest city in the world. Give me another drink; I am stuck with loving. The time has come to reveal my homes, to let my two lives out. My famous city has another beneath it full of myth, carved for one thousand years under its twin. I will take my leave of this whisky and replace it with another. There, delicious stuff. Now, how far had I got? Nowhere of course; we are at the beginning. What city is this? Nottingham. Why is it famous? For many reasons. What does it hide? Only another made of sandstone. Now look, my third drink is down the throat. Follow me under.

I was not born here, but my past will arrive later. First, the caves. A favourite entrance, for myself and the band of merry men who also know what I know, is the Peel Street Caves. If you hold close to these words you will learn new hiding places, silent places for thoughts to run, dark places for bodies to slide against other bodies. Here, torn from buff Sherwood sandstone, are great passages and arching rooms held by wide pillars. For hundreds of metres these caves pass under the city, and we choose to follow them. They have become galleries for our work, shelters for our weaknesses, chambers in which to rejoice and remember. Who are we? A genuine mish-mash.

Here is Black Boy, friend of mine sitting in the sand smoking heavily, one of Nottingham's own. He grew to his commanding height along the banks of the River Trent. He is obsessed with trees.

A little further under Peel Street and if you have quick eyes, they'll catch Corner Pin dashing around the pillars between the lights. He is a strange, fast friend and will only come to the surface during the night. This is because he has been hurt more than any of us.

And over there, either side of candles (which down here are a substitute for television), you can see Hickling Laing and his imaginary companion, Drury. They are both close to me because they too have come from a different city, and over time become stuck with loving this one. To be honest from the start, they were born in the same place as me and my story could easily be told through theirs. I think I'll let that happen, but later. There are more down here.

If you are careful and not easily distressed you can see, resting behind that pillar in the flicker of another candle, the owner of the Peel Street Caves, Rouse. A few facts about him: he is two hundred years old, therefore also owning a withered face that no-one wishes to see; he built these caves by taking ten thousand tons of sand to the surface, which is how he spent his youth; he is always angry; Rouse is not my friend.

Old Angel, who is neither, must be up on the surface. He is a reader of books, and though he does not write them, it was his idea that I should tell our stories. His reason? He is convinced the caves will one day be filled with concrete, covering us cowering within them. I do not think this will happen. Old Angel, I'll reveal now, is the most important part of my life. From the many hundreds who follow us down, there are perhaps three more who I want you to meet deeply.

Jalland is under the influence of many things. Whiston's mind is always made up. Plumtre is very rich.

I feel neglect because I've left myself to last. Who am I? All of these and a little more. My name is the most unusual in a city of unusual names. I am called Tigguacobaucc because I could not remember my real name when I arrived here, and that is what *here* is called: Tigguacobaucc. A replacement name. A city of two parts. An invention and a truth.

I have been many things but I am still young (though Rouse considers himself young). In one way I am now a singer and the diapason of my voice has been called astounding, but also a frustration. It seems I cannot quite decide at what pitch I should tell stories. I find it hard to trust myself because so many people have said they cannot trust me. This grows more complex when I can hear those voices clearly but am not sure if I should trust them. Situations that run in circles down here are known as The Rings. All of my friends suffer the weight of The Rings in their own ways. The Rings preclude happiness, and for that reason none or all of us are introspective.

This is not to say we are malingerers. We all work. I am a librarian in a library of medicine. My information is important, which makes me important. Perhaps some things need to be explained. Although Tigguacobaucc (the place) is basic, carved from sand and full of weirdness lit by candles, Nottingham, which sits on top of it, is not. Nottingham fuels the needs that any large city would feel obliged to fuel. One of those needs is for information concerning medicine, and when I am not underground I practice librarianship. I am happy only when I'm in a cave or a library.

I surround myself with musty walls and objects, whether above or below ground. This is one way for me to bear the weight of my Rings. I remember as a child spending hours finding places in which to breathe the unpopular air of corners. I never found myself lonely, as friends grew easily in the head. I wish I could recall my name as clearly as these memories; Tigguacobaucc is quite a mouthful. So habits do not die, and I've made a career and a life within pungence. This is what caves and libraries have in common: they are often corners. I love them both.

Sitting here in the Peel Street Caves with friends whose stories I've been advised to tell, I can almost begin to feel the air clearing, even this far underground. And that is the purpose of all their stories—to clear the air around me. Old Angel is worried about concrete filling our hiding places, but does he mean actual concrete or is he using concrete as an exaggeration of stale air. He is well known for his use of metaphor. Can he be trusted? Can I be trusted? Can we trust each other? Ah, The Rings. Either way, whichever way, under or over way, exaggeration comes in many forms and in all of them it is an underrated virtue. So in the end, at his very worst, Old Angel is merely a virtuous liar.

I won't give too much away about myself for two reasons: I don't remember many things from the time before I came here; and there is no point. Instead, follow me up to the surface again and we can continue the tour above the caves. You will be a yo-yo between Nottingham and Tigguacobaucc during these stories anyway; let's get some wind into the lungs.

If we were to take a taxi out of the City this is what we'd hear over the radio: Radford Chilwell Mapperley Mapperley Park Plains Meadows Basford Whitemoor Colwick Gedling Carlton Arnold Dunkirk University Sneinton Lenton Sherwood. The Rings for a Nottingham taxi driver are these names strung out endlessly over the airwaves. He cannot escape them, he can only make money from them. They are the *departments* of my adopted city. It has taken one thousand years for the city to sprawl out of the caves, away from the castle and over miles of ground once known as Sherwood Forest. It now sits in its own bustle and remarkable activity, either side of the Trent. All of this is good.

Only Rouse can remember Nottingham longer than a few years ago. He is difficult to talk to, and I hope one day to be rid of him.

From the air, and even more from the ground, Nottingham is as complex as any ancient settlement. The streets of Glasshouse, Huntingdon, Canal, Parliament (Lower and Upper), North Sherwood, and the roads of London, Derby and Mansfield are jacquards through centuries. These, coupled with the many Gates and Pavements, give the impression—and for the casual visitor the reality—of chaos. It will not be forgotten that beneath these common routes lies the maze of Tigguacobaucc. But do not worry, I will guide you through the twists and turns of these twin towns as well as I will through the stories of my friends. Only become wary if you find yourself following me up the paths of Nottingham's gardens. One in particular is full of lions.

Come then and feel this first night in my company. Walk with me through the streets and absorb Nottingham as I have done. See this city as a survivor, one of the few to remain important and of the even fewer to grow more beautiful. You will begin to recognise a livery possessed by an old place in the modern age; there is nothing fake here. This city will not play tricks (though its inhabitants might). I will interlineate the long story of the place. I will make it my purpose for a while to reveal secrets only an adopted son can reveal. I will promise you the fanaticism of a convert. My view of Nottingham is not that of someone who has become used to it; I see all as fresh. Guzzle yourself full of it, I hold nothing against greed. This town is yours for as long as you stay with me. Here is a gargantuan tin of red paint. And look what has been hiding behind my back—two brushes, one each to stripe the city with. Do not worry about being caught; everyone is at it. There are more artists here than the mind can contemplate, many people making their mark. And underground exhibitions stretching beneath the streets. Some of these were begun one thousand years ago, but the paint and scratchings are clear and are added to by my friends and others who know about Tigguacobaucc. This is not vandalism but evolution.

Youth is the largest group here, though remember how Rouse thinks of himself. We—those younger than thirty—are not recalcitrant, though our numbers would offer us that option. The authorities over Nottingham are acceptable. They do not stand between us and life. They have never sealed the favourite entrances to Tigguacobaucc. They are good listeners. So with all this in their favour we pay little attention to their peccadilloes. Sin is subjective in our town.

If you were to own a house on a hill in Nottingham, and awoke one morning to the bright sun, something would be missing. You would stand in large bay windows, searching the early mist and trees for what might be expected. You would spot one or two, they are not extinct. But it is not the familiar skyline of an aged English city. There are hardly any steeples.

The church has no grip on this place, though there is the rag-and-bone bric-a-brac selection of ways to worship Whatever, commonly associated with cities at the end of the century. But God, however he is painted, is no clarion here. Some of my friends feel sad at God's decline, in particular Drury, but as he is imaginary himself he is expected to relate to his own kind. Black Boy has turned his need for faith into a love of trees which, although my opinion counts for little, I admire. The person who hates God the most is Hickling Laing. This may surprise you as it does me, considering he imagines (and loves) Drury, but these are mysterious times. For my part, I am influenced only by my work.

A library will respond to palpation; I examine it for knowledge. My time is spent finding answers rather than asking questions. But once found I remember each answer; I do not search for the same answer twice. If librarians could live long enough they would gradually absorb the information held within their libraries. I would sit, an ancient man at a desk throwing answers from his head, a mirror of my library.

An invention and a truth. Is that possible? I will not live long enough to know.

Let us keep walking for a while longer, you and I. Tigguacobaucc, although submissive to its larger and more visible twin, is responsible for Nottingham's appearance. From that hypothetical house on a hill your eyes would not only search aimlessly for steeples, but also for tall buildings. This city does not grow upwards. Caves make it unsafe to build close to the sky. Instead, above and below ground, Nottingham has always grown outwards. In this sense it is the perfect place for Corner Pin, the best runner in Nottingham or Tigguacobaucc. He flits over the city with a disregard for amicability. I have never seen him meet anyone's eyes nor met his. His story is sad, but like all sad stories it has importance hidden within it.

Look, we have reached Canning Circus, and as you can see it is not a circus but a circle. The cars run around its outside and its centre is filled with pubs and shops and flats. The shops are mostly crammed with costumes and junkery to be bought or hired. I saw Dick Turpin, Bugs Bunny and an orange cow crossing the road here a few years ago, being careful of the traffic. Another shop holds hundreds of waistcoats. On one curve is Canning Terrace, a row of white houses standing like a great cake at the gates of a cemetery sweeping down from the Circus. The houses all have green doors. In the centre of the Terrace is a wide archway through which it is possible to see the gravestones. Above the archway is a clock, the hands of it inveterate in their journey. I cannot decide whether we should stand in the centre of the Circus and allow life to spin around us, or to find a seat on the edge. It would be more comfortable there but we should only see a part of the circle. I alternate between the two possibilities; there is both rest and excitement up here. In fact, this is one of Old Angel's most loved places on the surface, and as he was not in the Peel Street Caves earlier I am surprised we have not seen him. Another friend, Whiston, hates the Circus because he always knows exactly where he wants to be, but cannot be at the edge and in the centre at once. Despite Whiston's decisiveness I enjoy my time here; life seems less of a convolution when all around me is busy. I even stare through the Terrace archway with a light heart. Canning Circus proves that even in Nottingham, not every circular situation results in The Rings.

That is not the last you will hear of Canning Circus, but come now down Derby Road, past the shops stuffed almost onto the street with antiques, and into a secret place. Through a car park of smooth concrete lit orange, and out into this huge cylinder of stone twenty feet wide and reaching seventy feet up. Steps cling to the wall and spiral to the top, where the lack of roof gives us the stars. It is as if we have stepped into a telescope. And ahead of us, at a gigantic right-angle, a tunnel runs from the cylinder, as high as the cylinder is wide. The floor is a dry sand, safe from rain. The sand once held tracks of coach-and-fours, travelling from the City to The Park Estate at the end of the tunnel. Those contusions are rubbed away, but this is still a good place. The rock is the sandstone of our underground passages.

Jalland is often here, crawling from under one influence only to buckle beneath another.

Following the hooves of ghost horses we come into The Park. It sits as a private outskirt to the castle, an urbanity like no other. These are virtuoso red houses, each one a unique and polished performance. They reach in ever widening oval roads from the centre to the boundary of the estate. I walk here, treating each house as a book: bursting with information; an ocular wonder; shelved but accessible. I discovered a love in myself for architecture on the long quiet roads. These houses are aspirations. Only the rich can hold their keys, and to one of them Plumtre already does. I will not take you to see him yet, as I have warned you already about what lies inside his garden.

As you can see, we have almost emptied this tin of red paint. Just in passing, you realise by now only to believe some of the words I pass before your eyes; I don't want to blind anyone. Confusion can be very convincing.

I need another whisky and there are bottles in the caves, so I'll take you back to Peel Street. With any luck, Old Angel will have gone down and I can begin my promise to him. It is not a long walk if we use the caves. I hope something has been instilled in your heart for Nottingham. My evangelical attitude can be annoying, but it derives energy from a broken and lost background. I am replacing myself with new lives here. I cannot expect you to trust me considering the state I am in, but patience could be taken as a compliment. I understand that by running to Tigguacobaucc, by diving underground with these people, I am depriving myself of freedom. I will remain held by The Rings. But Old Angel is usually right, and I think he secretly believes that through telling the stories of my friends I might find my own story.

A person with no story is a diseased person. As is a person with too many.

Anyway, we have reached the Peel Street entrance so let us follow the steps to Tigguacobaucc. It is warmer down here. A womb of arches and pillars. Follow me through to The Hall, where my friends will sit with you. The sand walls can hold your back long enough for their stories. Ah, good, Old Angel has

descended and Corner Pin has slowed enough to hear. Black Boy is well sup-
plied with smoking material. Jalland, Whiston and Plumtre are determined to
survive the telling of their stories (though I hope we will come together as one).
Hickling Laing and Drury have extinguished the candles because, like television, they are a distraction. Give me another drink; I am stuck with loving.
Tigguacobaucc. An invention and a truth. Even Rouse has come out of his
shadows; I'll be glad to see the back of him.

chapter 2

the story of black boy

THE house stood itself slightly out-of-date and grand but jaded along the banks of the Trent. Black Boy spent his adolescence watching swans parade the river. He would stand facing the famous water from a balcony attached to the house. The balcony had for some reason an American influence: tatty wood with peeling paint, strong and pretty. Fortune had given him the room with doors to the balcony. It was out here, when it became late and Trent Bridge shone in its blue lights, that Black Boy drew on his first cigarette.

Since that wonderful private time, he sat in bed listening for even a tiny stir from the others. The house held many rooms holding many like him. He was not concerned with being seen; if that happened he'd decided to search for another corner. He simply did not want this routine upset by another boy having knowledge of it. Black Boy's primary instinct was that knowledge is power. Chance had given him a place to be alone, and he has spent much of his life coveting the balconies on other people's houses.

This house may have looked respectable to a danderer along the river, but it held boys with imaginations growing up, and therefore could not have been what it seemed. The boys kept a good garden. It appeared to have developed through the fingers of someone skilled in such matters, even warranting praise from The Old who stuttered past on Sundays dragging small dogs. Black Boy heard these remarks from his balcony but didn't care whether they amounted to compliment or criticism. He was not responsible for the plants. Another boy had green talent, and though this crowd possessed imagination it did not stretch to names. Green Boy looked after their garden.

Narcissism was Black Boy's hobby. He was busy with himself, and over his late teenage years a collection of mirrors grew across his wallpaper like algæ. Black Boy was, and still is, broken-hearted. This house ran in fact with boys without hearts. In a city as sopped by variety as Nottingham you might expect such a dispersion of lost loves. What is unusual is their flocking together. Though these boys had all cut themselves away from love, they had used different methods. Green Boy lost his heart to a flower. To be more specific, a bush coated in yellow flowers. The scent of the flowers surrounded him and his equally young lover for three years, but the bush lost its grip on life, and though Green Boy tried, he could not save it. Without the scent and regular propulsion of colour, Green Boy's mind became disharmonious. He had become so dependent on one plant he could no longer follow the seasons in its absence, and his lover left him, tired of being unable to plan further ahead than a few weeks. Green Boy was always in the wrong clothes.

But, as he has just reminded me, with his way of whispering through the wisps of smoke drifting between his teeth, this is Black Boy's story. For the benefit though of your ears, Black Boy is incapable of realising the power I hold. He would not exist if I did not require him as an ease to my own plight. Of course there are those who believe comfort prolongs agony. This can be diagnosed as a side-effect of The Rings.

You may be wondering how these boys could afford to live in what after all is an expensive part of Nottingham. A view of swans must be paid for. This is part mystery and part invention. To begin with they were all orphans, and though some of their parents were alive, these people are not worth my reflections. They were drowning so intimately in the problems of men and women they forgot their children. Each boy in the house was forgotten at a different age. Orange Boy, who was the closest to Black Boy, was the first to arrive at the house. In his own way he was a demon, though a gentle and good demon. He was extremely small and enjoyed sitting on Black Boy's shoulder advising him. Black Boy allowed this because Orange Boy always gave good advice, though for a while even he did not know about Black Boy's late outings to the balcony. Orange Boy paid for the house with the currency of persuasion. He had, so the story goes, asked for the house in return for a particularly indispensable piece of advice, and had received it. Since that day he had opened its doors to boys whose parents had forgotten them.

When Black Boy arrived at the house he had to describe to Orange Boy how he had become an orphan. The decision to leave home had not been easy, though getting out without his parents noticing had been. They were busy arguing. He had guessed that his father would himself leave very soon, and as he didn't wish to become a crutch for his mother's emotional strength he thought he would get out first. His mother didn't need support due to weakness, she simply could not support her own emotional obesity.

He was, as I've said, given by chance the room with a balcony. The room changed his life. None of the boys entered each other's rooms without permission. This agreement was reached quickly and easily because no-one had such privacy in their first homes. Black Boy and Orange Boy, though without hearts themselves, began to construct one in the dining room.

This room was directly below Black Boy's and so, like his, was at the back of the house facing the river. Black Boy was as skilled a constructor as he was a smoker, and it was with this skill he paid his keep. He could construct almost anything. When he first arrived Orange Boy was living a difficult life. Due to his lack of height, everyday activities were hard in a house built for ordinary sized people. Black Boy began in Orange Boy's own bedroom by chopping normal furniture into bits. For a few weeks the garden was covered with pieces of wood, much to the distaste of the passers-by. But gradually the large bedroom was filled with tiny furniture. Orange Boy was pleased with this and started Black Boy on a smaller version of the kitchen. Black Boy made small cabinets with wood left over from the bedroom. He even built a miniature cooker using a camping gas stove. These tiny rooms were added to over time, and it could be seen easily that Black Boy had greatly improved the life of Orange Boy.

Black Boy discovered in himself a passion for construction. It was more than a talent, it became his thoughts. He was unable to look at any constructed object, including relationships, without an unstoppable urge to become involved with that object, to transform. The difficulty for him and for those couples who came into his contact was the narcissism that drove the collection of mirrors across his bedroom walls. He could not help but create in his own image.

And though I can see you sitting comfortably with your back against our sandy walls, I can also see the need in your face to know how Black Boy looked back then, even before I had arrived in either Nottingham or Tigguacobaucc. Well, he had the appearance of one who watches rivers. This resulted in long brown eyes capable of sweeping over a room or body in ripples. These eyes could drown. He still possesses with them, as you will find should you want to when these stories are done. His hands were practised, streaked with veins from being almost constantly involved in processes of construction. The two fingers of his right hand gradually yellowed to their present condition from the cigarettes which kept him company on his balcony. Black Boy's body was as strong then as it is now. His face was built carefully. He used the material he had been given genetically and improved on it, losing weight to enhance cheek-bones, applying gloss to already full lips, and thinning the eyebrows with tweezers. When he had reached nineteen he looked better than anyone; at least that is what he thought. He also grew to a commanding height.

In fact Black Boy was one of his own first constructions. An invention and a truth.

Black Boy, Green Boy and Orange Boy were permanent residents in the house. Others came and went, chasing their lost hearts or frivolously wasting opportunities for contentment. One of these others was White Boy. His is a story in itself, but as he merely skimmed the surface of Black Boy's life so he shall skim this story. White Boy was a believer in many things but he owned no mirrors, so could never see himself for what he was: an object without reflec-tion. He was unique among the other boys in that he had never lost his heart. This did not mean he held one inside; rather he had never held one. The heart had been removed at birth by his mother and she had eaten it. Her husband was a dragon and she hoped two hearts would be safer than one. It may seem cruel for a mother to take a child in this way simply to protect herself from a man. It may seem cruel but it is certainly common. When White Boy had grown a little older he asked his mother where his heart was. She lied, instilling in her son the belief that God had requested this heart.

"In exchange," she said, "God has planned for you to become special. He assured me that one day you will become a prophet. This great thing will happen when you have found your heart; then you will be ready for such importance." His mother in her digestion knew of course he would never find it. She hoped that the search would keep him near her until the dragon she had married left for good. This plan did not work. White Boy arrived at the house by the river full of the thrill of the chase. He would sit talking to the other boys about belief. He described his life as a sacrifice, which Black Boy questioned because White Boy's life was led by his certain knowledge of a reward at the end. Black Boy, if he believed anything, knew that reward and sacrifice could not be used alongside one another. The only sacrifice in White Boy that Black Boy could be sure had happened was that of his common sense.

White Boy trusted his mother because what she told him made him feel important. This was a mistake. The other boys were going to dispose of White Boy in their own particular ways. Orange Boy hated him because White Boy firmly believed he was not in need of advice. Had he allowed Orange Boy to give him advice, it would have flowed gently into his ear from a small voice on his shoulder and probably changed his life. Black Boy advised Orange Boy not to attempt to sit on White Boy's shoulder as he was convinced White Boy consisted of nothing except empty space and points of light; had he tried he would simply have fallen to the floor. Black Boy proved himself right. One evening White Boy was stirring soup at the cooker. Black Boy quickly went and took a long mirror from one of his walls. He held it facing White Boy and it only reflected the cooker. White Boy was not in the picture, and from this moment Black Boy ignored him. White Boy only ever cooked soup and he had never been seen eating it, though he always brought empty bowls from his room. Black Boy thought that because White Boy was always running, never setting down roots, he had not developed the need to react to stimuli. Without these reactions he could not exist and so had no reflection. The greatest complexity inside White Boy was that he had become The Rings to himself. He was trapped by self-belief. He spent so much energy reflecting on his place in the world that his body emptied of energy and he lost his actual reflection. Green Boy wanted to use White Boy as compost, but by that time White Boy had already disappeared.

Although the house was theirs, running costs still intruded. But Nottingham proved a wealthy place for three teenagers with imagination. Any of the other boys left as soon as Orange Boy asked them for contributions. This habit upset him because he was certain that boys who had lost their hearts would quickly tire of chasing them, and wither in some suburb of the city. But no demon has ever been a charity, and Orange Boy did not intend to become the first. He himself did not work; there were few things he could reach. This is not to say he was not occupied.

He was called often in the night. In times of great personal need or stress he heard those who needed him and went to sit on their shoulders. It was an advantage being able to fly, for he could cross the city in minutes to whisper hope into the ears of those who had lost hope. To these people he was a marvel. There have always been enough people in Nottingham suffering under The Rings to keep Orange Boy in flight.

He came to my shoulder once, fluttering hope.

Green Boy delivered plants from ill health. He was a botanical Jesus. People, mainly The Old who had praised his handiwork, came across Trent Bridge to hand him their green-fingered failures. In a few weeks they would return to plants stretching with life, urging their leaves outwards, copulating with sunlight. Green Boy would be paid, but he also always took cuttings. Most of the garden at the house was grown from plants Green Boy had saved. The plants of The Old became like them, parents and grandparents. On Sundays with their dogs, The Old were admiring the grandchildren of plants long considered to be on the edge of death.

Though Green Boy and Orange Boy had lost their hearts, they had never misplaced a faith. They had never possessed one to lose. This was not the situation with which Black Boy struggled. When he escaped from the house where he was born in Sherwood, he had also run from the God of his parents.

For much of his life he had followed them. At seventeen he stopped. They and their friends were convinced this was an emotional decision, but it was not. Black Boy thought every minute of being awake. His brain had begun to open and crave. In the backstreet Sherwood house he got less and less sleep, for his eyes wandered during the days. They drew in so much information he was forced to process it far into the night. Each fact, each image, a statistic, a leg, a panel of glass, became undone in his mind. He dissolved everything he saw. His mind was a grey field littered with pieces of memories. Black Boy had become an apprentice to his trade: construction. He was in this state for a year before he moved to his room with a balcony.

An apprentice. For that year he deconstructed all he saw, though there was no reason he could feel for doing so. These were hæmal actions. For a while the parents did not notice a change in Black Boy, though slowly they saw him looking at objects for longer than they would themselves. But they soon grew used to this and continued battling. Black Boy had not yet had time to develop this urge to understand intricacies into a skill. It had not become useful. In his mid-teens he became interested in girls his own age, and true to form he took them apart. Once dissected he would leave them crying and move on to someone else. The rapidity with which he did this made him a hero amongst boys, and made girls nervous of him. Some of them decided to avoid him but most could not keep themselves away. He was simply too interesting. Other boys were not dealing with issues, they were not driven to understand, and girls liked someone who would think about them and who could use long words to describe their bodies. Black Boy was also, even then, very beautiful.

Black Boy was never a White Boy. He found it impossible to trust people who told him he was or would be important. Black Boy was the first misanthropist he had met. His distrust seared into every aspect of his life, and the deeper it reached the less evidence of God he found within himself. This operation into recesses of his body did not excite him; nor did it depress him. It was an addiction, and he could not stop himself. He often wondered if he could be trusted. What if one fine day he was examining himself and he scooped too much from his chest, his heart was lifted clean out into the air of Nottingham and it escaped, pounding out of reach?

This happened and his heart was lost.

Black Boy had shocked himself for the first time, but his convictions grew with the loss of his heart. Now he had a Grail. He would spend his life chasing this heart, and when he finally caught up with it, his brain would be strong enough to hold it close and use it correctly. For the rest of the year his deconstructive activities became manic.

His long eyes traversed girls' bodies. He intoxicated girls with attention, but they were never aware that the time he spent with them was for his own gain. Black Boy held his eyes before the breasts of these girls as his brain took in their details: the size of his own fist, the weight of ripe pears, the shape of blown glass. He implemented into his brain the depth of colour in the epicentre of nipples, and how this colour spun away in spirals towards their outer edges. He took steps away from the danger of these tornadoes. He held breasts in both hands and marvelled at their strength.

Black Boy's hands lowered themselves down the bodies of girls like great cranes. The muscle which had begun to expand on his arms was gentle, giving power to the hands which kneaded at their soft skin. He could hear the girls groan in his dreams, his hands making each larynx express guttural, primæval songs. He was a musician performing concertos on the female body and they too were his audience. His narcissism flowered on these beds as his own body was an encore.

He pushed his youth into the depths of girls. He dived into their hiding places and found warmth. Black Boy swam without clothes or oxygen, impressing this strange curved sex with his grace and the sustaining power of male lungs. His arms were a lariat around their lovers. There was no escape from him, his eyes took everything from each girl. They burst the length of their banks over girls' bodies and pulled them under into a strong current. This was not death. The girls were held in delight, they became safe. Their faces were immovable objects, full into his body in a state of entrancement. Their bodies, though held by his, were never still. They leapt upon him with the joy of grilse. Though caught they did not suffer.

The girls Black Boy examined in this manner suffered when he set them free. When he had listened to the sounds of their bodies he rid himself of them. Each one wept but he was already running to the next. They felt he had taken particles from every corner of what were once secret places. Black Boy had scoured and bloodied girls' bodies for an answer. Where is faith hidden?

From the bodies of girls he had learnt enough to extinguish God. A young man without a heart had to feed his need for tangibility. Compared to girls, God was a territory of impotence, though Black Boy had lost only the faith of the parents, not the desire for faith.

After this year of girls he decided to alter his life. First he moved to the house by Trent Bridge. Second he began to heed a demon. Third he smoked his first cigarette. Fourth he turned from girls to mirrors. At the age of eighteen Black Boy had cut himself away from love. He held his arms tight against the chest so nothing else could follow his heart into its distance. He stood on the balcony watching swans on the Trent. He inhaled smoke deeply. Life at the house became important to him, to all of them. Orange Boy enjoyed the fact he had obtained a house and made it available for boys without hearts like him. Green Boy's fingers were the digits of a sad magician and he expressed his love and emptiness by filling the garden. Black Boy had time and a place to think. It was here that his apprenticeship ended and he moved from deconstruction to construction. This is called *direction in life.*

The first mirror Black Boy was given was, in common with all his mirrors, in response to his looks. He had known his face could drag girls beneath the current of his eyes, he had not known it could give him himself.

Black Boy had been walking in Nottingham. He left the house and crossed Trent Bridge. Because time was not a problem he stopped halfway across and took the city horizons into the brain. North he could see the dome of The Council House and he walked in that direction, following London Road past the old station and into the shadow of the Lace Market. Black Boy felt fast and young. He almost ran up Hollowstone and Bellar Gate, then turned quickly into Barker Gate, Stoney Street and onto Broadway. He was suddenly surrounded by the real Lace Market. Great redbrick factories, elegant and high with dignity, stood around him. Black Boy loved what had been left here from the last century. Many of the buildings were now exclusive clubs. He had once dressed in black velvet and spent the evening in one, The Lizard Lounge, drinking vodka and watching girls. But most of these huge lace factories were shells. It was typical of Nottingham to have a beautiful and immaculate area of dereliction; this city even sold postcards of its disused quarters.

Black Boy moved from Broadway down St Mary's Gate, past Kayes Walk and St Mary's Church (wide and strong), and out onto High Pavement. He walked more slowly here, sucking architecture and finding it delicious. Then over Weekday Cross to Low Pavement, with a quick glance down Middle Hill to Canal Street and on into the city. As in many vintage towns, Nottingham is best viewed from street level with eyes up. Inside the square mile of its centre the buildings have grown like coral, teeming with life and alive themselves. It has taken many hundreds of years for them to become joined, entwined and dependent on one another. Their colours are greens and pinks and every stage of yellow. Their heights are competitive for sunlight, reaching to the surface of the city. But one will not detriment another; the smaller older buildings benefit from the shelter of new, faster growing varieties. Everywhere there are doors to anywhere. An old town holds many secrets.

Black Boy walked the full length of Low Pavement, then Castle Gate. He turned right and started up the noise of Maid Marian Way. He loved the traffic flowing against him until this feeling made nausea rise, so he took the subway and came up on the other side, for a second in full view of Nottingham Castle. Today this violent and decorative place was not where he wanted to spend time. He continued towards Derby Road and Canning Circus, where he had heard mirrors and costumes hung for a price.

That morning Black Boy, with a conviction he was giving birth, decided to become involved with himself further. To omit girls. To begin a prosthesis in the space left by his heart. To outrun his loneliness. His first construction would be a life, and to be accurate this life needed mirrors. Orange Boy had listened carefully to Black Boy as he covered his intentions, and advised if possible a gilded mirror—a mirror with a past, a mirror that could uphold lies. Black Boy, a boy without trust and therefore unstable, found the word *lies* too firm. He preferred to think of his body, his face, his truths as inventions. But the idea of preparing stares surrounded by gilt drove him across Trent Bridge to the antique shops on Derby Road.

And now he methodically entered them, finding them quiet and crammed. Cemeteries for objects. Black Boy had never been in rooms holding ugly delicacy before. None of those girls he had examined had been a combination of both. Most, due to his looks, had been the latter. And it was in the third shop that his looks saved him money. Downstairs there was a wall of mirrors. Each had a country of origin, a date of manufacture and a price. He could afford only one and he did not want it. The frame of this mirror was blue, harsh, volatile, made in Iceland in 1984. Black Boy wanted old gold.

He had tested the rest for an hour, staring into each one, raising his eyebrows, pulling his cheekbones high, pushing the lips towards their reflection. Exaggeration comes in many forms and in all of them it is an underrated virtue. Black Boy could be seen in his blinkered youth by a woman. She had watched him for this hour, her only movement being to check her pulse occasionally from the wrist under bracelets of great age. The woman loved Black Boy from the first time she saw him see himself. Five minutes after the hour had finished Black Boy had promised to return in exchange for the mirror he most desired. That was all, no charge.

Before walking back south of the river, Black Boy visited the costume shops on Canning Circus and chose some black clothes. This time using up some money.

So Black Boy's direction in life began with a mirror. He never looked back. Into his room went this first mirror, and it was followed by others. Neither did he need the attentions of the woman he had promised to reveal himself to. In Nottingham there are plenty of shops full of mirrors being sold by faint-pulsed women, and Black Boy found promises easy to make.

The collection grew with his self-interest. His loneliness receded with each newly framed reflection, and should he ever become bored with the view he always had his balcony and the swans. Black Boy began to develop regularities. Like all born smokers, he was habitual, possessive of his time, and enjoyed the night. Stars flow in the eyes through smoke. Alone and outside, Black Boy would look up down the length of an entire cigarette, letting the sky swirl. He could control the stars with the speed of his exhalations, making them vanish behind fast smoke or glint through rings. He saw the stars and felt them, imagined them tipping a great point of light onto his skin. He was in pain but he knew the distance this star had travelled to prick him; he believed the science of light and speed were trying to wake him up. He was stroked by physics.

Inside his chest Black Boy felt the absence of his heart, but still the response was mirrors. By the age of twenty-one he had coated the walls of his room with his own face. The room echoed every movement made by his now muscled body. His talent for construction had not neglected the physique. Black Boy's narcissism was now growing from the neck down like scales. With the addition of two German full length mirrors made in Munich in 1923, he became as fascinated with his body as he had always been with his face. Perhaps by extending the search for faith below the neck he would close on that Grail. Black Boy's torso and limbs were now an incentive. He would lie in bed waiting for sleep, excited by what he could see again in the morning. His was not a questioning self-awareness; instead it revelled. Black Boy did not find himself disturbing. This was a voyage of discovery, a solo exploration of his veneers. Despite the occasional deep touch of stars, he was merely examining skin. The mirrors made sure of that. But they above all could not hide him from himself, and they framed ferociously. Mirrors were his machismo.

Faith, though, still teased him and he was empty. Orange Boy advised him to construct a heart. It was during the research for this ambitious construction that I first met Black Boy. He needed medical details and my library was the obvious source. I had only lived in Nottingham for a short time and back then was without a name. I had run to the city from many things, and the trauma of leaving what I had left had removed much from me, not least my name. In Black Boy I saw familiar needs. He searched the shelves of my library like a shark, gliding, banking, turning effortlessly. His were the movements of hunger and purpose, and I could do nothing but help someone kindred. Black Boy's first questions were full of energy but without skill. He had no language prepared for the complexity of medicine. All he knew was that he was building a heart and he needed a blueprint. I did not possess his manual dexterity but I could speak the language, so we began to work together. I first provided him with information on coronary anatomy, and encouraged him to think of the heart in angiographic views, to think in great detail. This took time, but he gradually recognised the right and left coronary systems at both right and left anterior oblique views. The branches of the two principal coronary arteries: sinoatrial, lateral, obtuse marginal, medial circumflex, circumflex, atrioventricular and septum expanded in Black Boy's brain until he could begin to construct a heart in his living room. I had been wondering for some time where he intended to gather the materials needed, and he told me these were given willingly to him by many broken-hearted women. By the strike of his looks I found this easy to believe. An invention and a truth.

The first time I was taken to Black Boy's house by Trent Bridge I admit I found his life strange, but no more strange than my own had become. I arrived there one Friday after my staff had gone and I had locked the library. We ate soup made from ingredients grown by Green Boy, then cleared a large table in the living room and started to build this heart. I had brought some relevant books but found we rarely referred to them. Orange Boy did not grasp the language of medicine that Black Boy and I were using throughout the construction, but for a demon without his own heart he had a remarkable understanding of how the object would work in practice. The many cries from the human heart that he had answered had given him insight beyond the mechanical. And with

Green Boy feeding us well we became a team working into the night. At around midnight, Orange Boy perched on my shoulder and lifted his ears upright to listen to the city. He was intent and soon apologised, flying over the Trent to someone he said was in great distress. We had worked for six hours on the smaller aspects of the heart and decided that for now we would stop. I was too exhausted to leave so I stayed and entered Black Boy's room for the first time.

We did not sleep. We sat on the balcony watching swans and smoked through conversation. I told him of my love of whisky and we drank some. He explained how to obtain a large collection of mirrors on a tiny budget. We tried to analyse the overwhelming nature of The Rings. We found common ground in our needs, and were glad to be in Nottingham. Black Boy told me how he delighted in the Lace Market, its curves and heights, and I listened because I had not thought I would ever meet another person who could be moved by buildings as I was. After a few hours the wind came off the Trent a little stronger and we went inside to Black Boy's room of mirrors. The talking continued and it was the beginning of friendship. Gradually sleep became the strongest force and we drifted down into it, surrounded by our reflections.

Over many similar weekends both the heart and our friendship grew in complexity. Green Boy would provide fresh food and late into the night Orange Boy heard and responded to those who needed him. The heart, though, became our emblem. It pulled us all into its intricacies. During those nights Black Boy told me of mirrors and girls, of cigarettes and parents, of the march of swans, and eventually of faith and its loss.

God had once been tangible to him. But this God, the God of his parents, became a procedure, a guide book. It was a God interpreted to him by his mother and father; they were its priests and intermediaries. The more they came between Black Boy and God, the further God receded until his parents drew a full and permanent eclipse across his faith. It was in this darkness that Black Boy had examined his heart and lost it. The experience allowed Black Boy to see through the trust White Boy had in his mother when she told him he would be a prophet. Despite an encompassing distrust, Black Boy believed the only truth was that Truth could not be imparted by someone else. So ran his grand narcissism. Mirrors became a fervent and honest direction.

The house by the Trent began to change him though. He found Green Boy articulate in his constant care for their stomachs. He already knew that Orange Boy would advise him correctly on how to cope with The Rings. Black Boy was powerless to halt a trickle of trust developing. He was discovering friendship. Inside his dark body a kind of faith was being slowly rekindled.

The building of the heart continued. After a time it existed enough for me to warn of the diseases that could strike it. I carried books over Trent Bridge that told of the frailty of hearts. All of us knew this instinctively, but we learned the details and signs. One book described angina pectoris, a central, crushing chest pain which may radiate to the jaw, neck or one or both arms. It is precipitated by exertion, anxiety, cold weather and heavy meals. It is relieved by rest and nitrates. Another book contained words on myocardial infarction, the death of heart muscle. The pain in this case is usually of greater severity and duration than in angina, and associated with great distress. To watch here are the painless infarcts which can kill in silence. This is often a cause of death amongst The Old. Black Boy listened to these warnings, but said there was no pain described here that he had not felt himself, even without a heart. But I could see he began to take more care than usual in his work.

As the heart came nearer to completion a twinge of calm fell over the house. We all began to expect the heart to dehisce, but in a way not damaging to itself and yet transformative to ourselves. We were all in need.

One evening Black Boy and I took a late walk down Trentside. Across the river from the balcony the memorial to Nottingham's War Dead haunts the horizon. We had both been there but never together. Our friendship had developed enough to allow for silences, so we walked to it. I followed Black Boy down from the balcony, through the garden, over the small wall and out onto the riverside path. It was night, though a big city night, hung over by orange from the many thousand street lights. Trent Bridge cast its familiar blue reflection on the water and we walked towards it, careless of the silence between us. At the river's edge a number of large boats were moored, lighting the steps from the path down to the water from their cosy rooms. Inside one a couple sat facing each other playing cards, rocking slightly on the current and enjoying life. Black Boy saw me drawing conclusions from the scene. We moved onto damp grass and past County Hall, its green roof clashing against the city sky. To the right across a marble of roads sat Trent Bridge cricket grounds, but we turned left onto the bridge itself. The noise of traffic occupied us until we had crossed and gone through the huge gates onto Victoria Embankment. The width of the road struck us and we walked under the great trees that line it. Their roots, spread around each base, looked like the calm, poised fingers of a snooker player's hand cradling a cue. It was not possible to tramp by such old life, and we stopped. The silence was broken when Black Boy asked me if I had ever looked at trees with all my brain. I had not.

Black Boy became animated and his long eyes were wide with energy. He forgot the heart for the first time in weeks, pulling his fingers gently down the crocodilian bark. He held his nose against the girth and smelt this giant. Inside, he said, were rings; but unlike The Rings that made us suffer, these rings shot nourishment through the height of the tree to its leaves. Black Boy described the life of trees as immeasurably slow stretches. From underground each new plant would push to the surface, then over many of our lifetimes it would reach for the sun. We cannot follow the progress of an individual because we lack time. To chart one tree means passing its location to another human who will return years after us and glimpse, only to pass to another person and another. The individual grows further out of reach and wider, charting in rings within its body. Death will come eventually as with all life, but if left untouched an individual makes a mockery of our centuries. Black Boy told me of Major Oak in Sherwood Forest who has lived for almost a millennium. Black Boy spoke with the conviction of the converted.

We walked further along the Embankment to the War Memorial, which sat wide and silent over Memorial Gardens. That was the first evening winter had made any impression on the city. There was little wind but the temperature made the mind cower within the skull, alert and timid. The large shallow pool in the shadow of the Memorial was still, preparing itself for the worst. Water had no protection from the air. Black Boy sat on the pool's surrounding wall and lit a cigarette. His smoking silhouette profile made him seem like a famous poet, lonely and concerned only with his loneliness. This was a kind of beauty. For a moment I stepped back and thought I saw him as a creature of my own imagination. He was distant, and so was the world in which we found pain and comfort. The heart nearly built in the living room, the demon on our shoulders, the individuality of trees and the extraordinary gardener. All of it briefly over-whelmed my own order and understanding, my life appeared to limn reality, not life*less* exactly, and not without truth, but an invention.

I breathed hard into my gloves and walked back up to the Trent. Black Boy followed me. We crossed the suspension bridge and made it sway by jumping on the wooden slats. There were swans clumped under us on the water, quietly bobbing and on their marks to run from winter. From the suspension bridge it was only a short walk to the house, and we slung ourselves into its warmth. Before sleep, Black Boy told me that the River Trent derives its name from the Celtic word *Tristanton*, meaning trespasser, due to a long history of bank-breaking. He told me the river had taught him how to tug girls towards him. I responded by believing every word he said.

The walk remained in Black Boy's brain. He had for the first time fully seen a life that was not a girl, not a reflection in a mirror, not one laying claim to being God. That night he became obsessed with trees. But this was not to the neglect of the heart. Orange Boy now spent hours whispering details of love and lost love into Black Boy's construction, though he never ignored a call from the city. Orange Boy kept the secrets revealed by these callers hidden, but he said that for a few weeks most of his calls had been coming from one person. He had discussed ways through the jungle of this person's difficulties and suggested to him that all of us should meet. The person agreed and gave his permission for Orange Boy to reveal his name. His had been the call answered by the demon that night we had begun to construct the heart. Orange Boy said his friend was in constant distress, could run faster than he himself could fly, and called himself Corner Pin.

A few days later the heart was finished. The last parts to be attached were the pulmonary veins and arteries, the givers and takers of life, and Black Boy sank into a chair which cushioned his exhaustion. Orange Boy whispered final, ancient advice down the thick aorta and the heart began to beat. We opened wine around it and stood listening. There was no need for blood. This heart did not exist to power an organism; it had been constructed as a phantom organ for the residents of the house. The boys without hearts now had one they could call their own.

Black Boy did not feel its effects immediately. It took him time to realise the link between the construction of the heart and his insight into the individual lives of trees. But this link was apparent to the rest of us. Black Boy had in his own way found a faith.

The religion of his Sherwood parents was distant though. He did not worship or praise trees as they did God. He had no spiritual motive, only admiration. Black Boy remembered one of the girls he had swept away telling him of some-one in Nottingham who held lions beneath his garden. He found trees to be the King of Plants, as lions are of Beasts. Just as the stars stroked him with physics, so trees towered over him in their huge biology. Science had grasped him firmly in its primæval, mortal hands. God drew his last breath in its grip.

Black Boy was born to love trees; he could sway in the wind. His height had been an afterthought of his body. Since coming to the Trent he had grown taller than anyone he had seen. The trees sensed this and accepted him. He could reach high bark without a damaging climb, without inflicting pain. We spent many more nights through that winter wrapped on the balcony. For a few days the river almost froze into a snake of ice, letting snow rest over its flow. There were no birds, and The Old kept themselves indoors. Green Boy's garden protected itself by turning into sticks, waiting for new months. Black Boy and I cultivated a full friendship, warming the winter with talk. I was happy that the heart worked as it should. I was happy that trees welcomed him. I remained in a kind of sadness because I could not remember my name.

The ice cracked slowly on the path. It stopped snowing. Small birds filled their throats and began to raise a warmer sun. Winter was collapsing. Orange Boy no longer returned from night flights with ice on his wings. Green Boy coaxed tips of leaves out of every nervous plant. The library became a different kind of refuge, not from weather but from an increasing sense that I had mis-placed most of myself. I had always owned a heart, and understood how to maintain and use it. But a name… I lived in this great city without a name.

As Nottingham crawled into spring Black Boy felt through his constructed heart a sense of worth where he had formerly felt only loss. He never denied memories, even those of God. Under his parents in Sherwood he had conducted a relationship with something insubstantial. He could not wipe out the many times spirituality seemed within reach. Before his own heart had leapt from his chest he knew it had rustled to the voice of this God. He would not deny experience, but with the courage shown by all atheists, he decided to understand his memories.

A kind-faced man had become involved in Black Boy's confused early teens. The man was tall and rich. He was in charge of a hospital but could not distinguish between those inside its walls and those outside. To him, all people were sick. He saw Black Boy's ordinary adolescent struggles as battles between good and evil. Black Boy was usually too weak from the turmoil in the brain to argue, and it was easy for the kind-faced man to take him down to London for weekends. Black Boy and the man always slept in the same hotel room, which made Black Boy feel uncomfortable. He was always asked gently to undress under the man's kind glare. His body, though young, was already strongly male in its beauty. The man never touched but was rewarded for his kindness.

Black Boy spent many evenings in the man's simple house, for the man gave away most of his money to far countries lilting with hopeless people. The man was not evil but he suffered like everyone beneath The Rings. His suffering was of the cruellest type. He had convinced his brain, a thing of electricity and chemistry, that it could commune with non-existent beasts. God quickly became the man's only true friend. God would not answer back. The Rings held him tight in their orbital motion. He circled his deepest, most honest desires, unable to touch but earning enough money to bring them into sight.

The evening that still haunted Black Boy took place in the man's sparse front room. In it sat three musicians, Black Boy and the man. The musicians tracked a similar orbit of The Rings as their host. Black Boy could remember dim lights and a strong smell of expensive coffee. Much of the time was spent in good conversation and laughter, for though these men suffered they did not recognise their suffering and were happy. All evenings at the man's house ended in prayer. Black Boy felt little of the firm presence of God that the man spoke of during these prayers, but he enjoyed the undeniable sense of peace. The outside world was disinterested. But that night was not private, it was communal and oppressive. The musicians in prayer transformed from joviality to attack. They told Black Boy the man had asked for their help, and that they were here now to pray over him. Black Boy looked across at the man, who smiled and suggested he fall to his knees before God. All four men began praying loudly for God to end the struggling within Black Boy. They turned their voices into instruments and sang and played in strange tongues. Though Black Boy's eyes were shut, he felt the sweat of these men striking his head. The onslaught continued for many minutes, until the men fell around Black Boy and writhed in what they described later as ecstasy. The only emotion Black Boy felt was a repellent fear. He did not feel 'washed', as the men had called upon God to do. While on his knees he had imagined his ribs as a strong fence, protecting his heart from dangerous words. He was scared and never went back.

Orange Boy, Green Boy and I listened to Black Boy's memory beside him on the balcony. This was the first night he had allowed everyone up here. It was also the first time Black Boy had opened himself fully before us. The swans had returned to their parade ground and the Trent looked wide and important. The Old were passing the garden again, though some familiar faces had succumbed to Winter. The trees responded to Spring in a way similar to Black Boy, resuming their stretch for the sun. They budded like him in the precious air. By delighting in the growth of trees Black Boy learnt that science could fend for itself; it needed no God. By building a heart rather than chasing his own, Black

Boy found security. By allowing others onto his balcony, he cultivated friendship. Black Boy had stumbled upon faith in earth, not in heaven.

But under Nottingham, Corner Pin ran like a mad thing.

Orange Boy arranged a meeting with his strange fast friend, and one night told Black Boy and me to meet him on Peel Street. He had decided that because I was sad, this would allow me to drift into Corner Pin's story with ease. For though Orange Boy had perched on many sad shoulders, he warned us that the shoulders of Corner Pin were slumped at the saddest angle. He had also watched Black Boy's progress away from girls and mirrors and God, happy now to consider him useful to others. Black Boy's narcissism was dispelled by the wisdom of a demon. It was, after all, Orange Boy who had first suggested the construction of a heart.

It was late when I arrived at the entrance to the Peel Street Caves, and Black Boy, with Orange Boy hovering beside him, was waiting. The nights had become warmer. This was to be my first descent into Nottingham's caves, though Orange Boy knew them well. He told us that these particular caves were still owned by the man who built them. A man called Rouse who had hacked away for sand two hundred years ago. This man also owns a withered face and is always angry. We would not meet him that night.

The steps down to the caves ten metres beneath the city first wind back on themselves and then zig-zag to the floor. They are the caves you are now sitting in for these stories. I hung back from the dim light as Orange Boy flew around the many pillars calling for Corner Pin. Black Boy walked further into the cave, letting his long eyes adjust to life at this depth. He appeared even taller in the low rooms. A lithe figure shot past him and into darkness, quickly followed by Orange Boy, who fell to the floor exhausted. Just as he was about to speak the figure returned, but this time halted before us. His eyes were black from time in dark places. His skin looked smooth and almost luminescently pale. He was breathless and his young face contorted with wrinkles. Behind this face lay such obvious pain that Black Boy and I sat in the sand. The caves were quiet until the figure began breathing more easily, and introduced himself as Corner Pin.

chapter **3**

the story of corner pin

H

E had not always dwelt in dark places. Corner Pin had been forced into it. Tigguacobaucc, the underground city of sand, accepted him as someone in need of shelter. That night, when Orange Boy first allowed us to meet him, Corner Pin had met very few people he could trust and many he could not trust. Orange Boy was the first to hear his story and you, sitting under Nottingham with us, you I hope will be the last. Corner Pin is twenty-three years old and has been running since he was seventeen. His face though, screwed as it is in physical and mental exertion, is the face of someone many times older.

He has been hurt more than any of us. His story is sad.

Black Boy understood Corner Pin from the beginning because parents were the problem for them both. But unlike Black Boy, Corner Pin's father ran first. His father did the leaving.

In the old days Corner Pin lived in a large house with a mother and a father, and also with an elder brother. He was close to his elder brother because only two years separated them. In this house the family was not rich, but Corner Pin and his elder brother Car were happy. They played in the huge garden. The garden was two hundred and seventy feet long, long enough for the brothers to be unaware of what happened in the house between their parents.

This was the first malady.

There was no violence; the sickness of their parents ran deeper than fists. Though God yet again sat ringside washing his hands, Corner Pin and Car have only happy images of being younger; they knew of none of this until it hit them.

The parents were married in a big English city where the steam and clatter of industrialisation was loud enough to cover the mistake they had made. When they left it was too late for friendship; they had become strangers. Corner Pin handed a poem to me to read into this story, and here it seems to fit.

Too Low For Radar by Corner Pin

Lassoed and struggling in the place where years ago
my parents could be found taxiing for take-off,

enhances those old photographs of them together.
Mum teaching forty kids, young all of them. Dad

messing about with engineering of some kind. An
apprentice who decided to exchange the spanner for

the pulpit and started to fiddle instead with the
mysterious workings of God. Here their flying began.

Birmingham was the last place my parents were
young and maybe—I'll say it—grounded.

Then the twenty-year ascent of marriage which I will
not call, by turning turbulence into, poetry.

But flight is not the natural state for such large
animals as parents, who parachute children to the

ground, while through the buffeting of wind and other
forces lose altitude themselves. Flight is an achievement

copied from the more naturally accomplished, and
like all science someone is left roped to the ground.

And here I am on the old runway, waiting for news
of parents circling somewhere, too low for radar.

And strange breeds strange. Inside the mind of this poet is someone careful with words because he knows the power they hold, said or unsaid. But the Eden behind his house protected Corner Pin and his elder brother from words sparking away between their parents. Corner Pin is the product of two people unable to love one another. The house, with this family in it, sat south of the Trent in an area of Nottingham called West Bridgford. But love was not absent. The house was halfway along Pierrepont Road, settled and semi-detached. Some might say that this road is in Lady Bay, not Bridgford, but only those who care. There was no love from parent to parent, and only a tiny portion from father to sons, but from the mother to her boys love flowed incessant.

And the size of things is what youth is all about.

The garden began in a patio, unkempt with weeds surfacing through the gaps between stones. It was large though, large enough for Corner Pin and Car to develop military strategies with plastic soldiers across it. The terrain became miniaturised, a tiny scene of death and triumph, an echo of the house. From the patio and down one huge step, there was a stretch of grass. At one side of the stretch was an old white giant of a sink, flooded with parsley. It was on the edge of the sink that Car had once force fed his brother a banana. It was on the edge of the sink they had laughed so hard that Corner Pin had to fire the chewed fruit out of his mouth onto the grass where it sat for hours like a big yellow lump of fun.

From the grass and taking the full width of the garden, the father and mother grew raspberries. Gardening was a rare joint venture. To protect the red fruit from birds, the whole plot was covered in green netting like a marquee. The net was supported on four sides by seven foot poles and a door had been cut into it on one side. The raspberry plants were shouldered in rows. One evening a blackbird managed to enter the net and flew madly, crashing into its sides and roof. Freeing the bird was a rare joint venture.

Past the net another, this time wilder, stretch of grass bedded two old apple trees. They produced small sharp fruit which were often caught by the mother before they hit the ground and crushed into pies. A wasp, disturbed by its apple-burrow falling towards earth, once flew out of the apple and between Corner Pin's teeth before stinging his tongue. He screamed and then curled in a corner.

After the apple trees vegetables grew. Many types were there but especially potatoes.

God's family is a global family and the house held visitors to England from different countries. The father of the house was a vicar, blessed by God to become obsessed with himself. During the spring and summer he could be seen from the house digging potatoes at the far end of the garden, wearing a white handkerchief knotted at all corners on his head. He would push hard into the ground with a spade and flick soil and potatoes over his shoulder to be sorted apart. Corner Pin and Car often came from school and looked out from their room to see this effort going on. Despite everything it was comforting to see him there, to know he had not left. But for a few weeks the father had not been in the house. The boys did not know why and they were not told. Instead of him, a vicar from Norway was staying. He was big and nice, and from a distance— though only from there—he could be mistaken for the father. Corner Pin has a memory that he came home from school during his father's absence and looked down the garden where a man was digging with a cornered handkerchief on his head. Corner Pin ran and ran to the vegetable plot calling his father who turned and spoke through a Norwegian smile.

This was the second malady.

Beside the plot was a wide and tall heap of compost, high enough for things to exist and experiences to happen behind it. Corner Pin and Car discovered that behind the rot a giant green sabre-toothed rodent had made his lair. To this creature, children were nothing but food and though the brothers never saw it with open eyes, they could feel it on their necks. Fear did not stop them going there. Sex made sure they did. Compost is the perfect castle from which to experiment with your own body or the bodies of friends. Car remembers most clearly a discussion with a friend who said his much older brother had hair around his cock. Car could not then imagine what this would be like, but he also could not stop trying to imagine. He has never forgotten that afternoon.

And the garden was surrounded on all sides by an eight foot hedge. And it was thick and beautiful. And the garden was with form and was full, and a summer light seemed to be permanently upon the face of it. And the spirit of God moved among the boys and the raspberries and all the plants and birds. Even in the house where love was spoken of but untouched, God was called before every meal. And before sleep Corner Pin and Car mentioned small things to him about their lives and hoped he had not been looking behind the compost. And in the other room the parents slept together at a great distance and the father prayed to be given more foreign trips, and the mother pushed her little head into her pillow and asked for it all to end.

Her most frequent endearment for the boys was to call them *lover*. This came from the bottom of her Devon heart, for she was a West Country girl. They both liked hearing it and did not notice that in this small way they had replaced their father. But she cared deeply for them. They were fed fresh food from the garden and clothed enough not to stand out in school and hugged enough to feel that their mother's tiny body was on their side. The mother's body drew its powerful energy from the knowledge that its partner was a recidivist. The father was an habitual and brilliant liar. The father was also until later in life a minister of the church who preferred the mother to keep a hat on her head and her mouth shut.

He had begun as an apprentice engineer, young and without significant dreams, but a dreamer nonetheless. It can only be guessed why engineering lost its potential to fulfil this man's small dreams, but it did and he dropped it in a pile with the tools of the trade. The tangibility of steel is probably to blame; it was too definite and cold. So instead of metal he chose God, and followed him until God had placed a collar around his neck. This collar, white against smooth grey suits, was all Corner Pin's father needed to live. But this is not to say that it was honourable or simple.

Engineering is complex work but it can be understood. Corner Pin's father did not want to involve himself in a subject with clearly defined points of entry and re-entry, specific drivers for specific screws. God provided him with tools he could not hold and bits of belief that were impossible to piece together. And this was love.

And this was love because it was what he wanted: unending complexity; a world where paint ran in swirls, not taut between numbers. These saturating flowing colours where he hid his own belief made his brain feel intelligent; it must be so to even attempt to live with unproof. And so the small man from a small place feels big because he is friends with God.

In terms of sermons things were different. Corner Pin's father was a great preacher. He could make old ladies jump in their seats, he could stand hair on the arms of strong men, he could terrify and delight children. The strange and complex world of his own belief was portrayed to the congregation as simple and secure. He was so brilliant and exciting and safe up there in the pulpit, jacket off, walking easily around, shouting then whispering, watching his watch with light pouring onto him through the long church windows, that only from that distance between pew and pulpit did Corner Pin and Car feel he was there for them. On stage he was a real father.

This was the third malady.

Both boys can remember their father saying loud from his vantage point, *"I love my children. I am proud of my boys. I would die for them."* Both boys can remember that it was only in front of a few hundred people that they heard these words. Their father did not hold them at night and whisper words just for them. When they got older they realised that anyone can say anything with an audience.

Still, this was life and they loved it. Every fourth Sunday was communion, when their father took control of old symbols with old words. In their father's church after the main service, the congregation were invited to stay in their seats or leave. No one ever left. He was too good to miss. He came down from the pulpit to a large pine table with a white cloth as a diamond across it. On the cloth rested four silver plates full of little squares of white bread. Beside the plates stood four trays specially cut to hold many tiny goblets. The goblets brimmed with blackcurrant juice. Corner Pin and Car would watch as their father hovered his thick gardener's hands over these things. He stood behind the table, flanked by two church elders on his side. The elders took turns to pray for the feast and to thank God for his goodness. Then they each lifted a plate of bread and methodically walked through the congregation, offering pieces only to those who had been Born Again and who had received the Lord Jesus Christ personally into their hearts. Each person held the bread until the elders returned to their minister, who took a piece himself and lifted it high proclaiming it to be the body of Our Lord Jesus Christ, broken for all who accept him. He and the congregation put the bread in their mouths and savoured its dull perfection. After a couple of minutes of bowed silence the elders stood again, but this time offered a portion of blackcurrant juice to everyone before returning to their minister. He then held his little goblet high and thanked God for the precious blood of Our Lord Jesus Christ, shed for all who accept him. And there would be more silence.

And Corner Pin can remember those silences. In his memory communion services were always conducted in bright sunshine. The church was wide and full of gentle people who were interested in him and asked him how school was going. The sun would throw itself onto his father and all those gathered under him. Sitting there in the warmth of the light, he would rest his head on his mother's arm and think of the good food she had prepared. Often visitors came back for Sunday dinner and he would look forward to having others in the house.

Then he and Car would have a free afternoon in the garden before the evening service, or sometimes everyone would go for a walk. Nottingham has many places suitable for Sundays, but the boys' favourite was Wollaton Hall, set in hundreds of acres of rollable hills and climbable trees. The grounds held a huge lake where Car would sit for hours bird-watching and ticking species off in his notebook. Car can remember trips to Wollaton Hall clearly too, especially during summer. The family would drive out of West Bridgford and through Lenton, the big student area of Nottingham, where as he got older he would pay closer attention to groups of male students playing football without their shirts. One of Car's most guilt-ridden prayers was to ask God for sunny Sundays.

This, though, was not a malady.

Sometimes after the evening service Corner Pin and Car would persuade their mother to invite people back for supper. This she would do gladly because she knew her husband would continue his performance if they had visitors, and would therefore not slump in a corner and sulk all evening. Supper was wheeled in on a hostess trolley; sandwiches and cakes with plenty of tea. It would usually be a middle-aged couple for supper. The woman helped Corner Pin's mother in the kitchen while the man allowed himself to be toured through the father's vast collection of theological books. These evenings were always fun; the women enjoyed preparing food and didn't mind not being included in the serious discussion of church business that the men were enjoying. Corner Pin and Car were allowed to stay up a little later than usual, but loved these evenings even after they had gone to bed, because lying in the room they shared they would both drift into sleep listening to the calm murmur of adult voices downstairs.

And the size of things is what youth is all about.

Corner Pin rarely slept through the night without waking himself and his brother with his screams. He would dream of uncertainty and the fear of it would throw him awake. His mother hid the suffering inflicted upon her by the father, but like many children Corner Pin was registering his mother's unhappiness without intention. Corner Pin always was a creature of premonition. He never dreamt images, only what he later called rhythms and even later, observed during his life in Tigguacobaucc, The Rings. In some ways people believed him to be blessed from God, especially those in the church. But most who are blessed in the eyes of others are damned in their own. His ability not to see but to feel into the future would eventually send him underground. And running underground at speed as he does now pushes pain through his legs like an injected drug through the blood. It hurts him. But his premonitory Rings haunted him in the tainted idyll of his childhood. Those legs which would later rush him beneath Nottingham would wake him in agony, and his screams passed fear on to Car like a baton.

Car would be woken by his brother lying only a few feet away in another bed. Their room was very large and looked out across the back garden, which meant no street lights shone onto them at night. It was a dark room. On the floor was a boisterous carpet of huge brown flowers on a green background. The walls, like all the walls in the house, were papered with wood-chip and in the boys' room this was painted white. Corner Pin and Car had been taught by their mother to treat belongings as precious. Their room was usually immaculate, and though the boys didn't keep toys on display everything was used properly. All toys were treated as treats. Sometimes friends came over to play and often damaged Corner Pin's and Car's possessions. This would later make them both cry.

Gradually, although both boys were popular in school, they dispensed with many friends who would never become close anyway. They both took this technique to extremes when they became adults, until Corner Pin ended as the fastest runner through or under Nottingham, and Car became... well, no-one seems to know what happened to Car except that he returned to Nottingham after leaving it. There were, however, two children who lived in the house a couple of doors down Pierrepont Road who were glad to join Corner Pin and Car in their giant garden. Their own father was a builder who filled their garden with dangerous machinery and massive piles of slowly drying concrete. Their garden looked like a wasteland, while Corner Pin's and Car's garden, with its green marquee and savage sabre-toothed rodent, appeared a challenging paradise. The children were brother and sister and were called Saint Steven and Saint Joan, named after famous people they had not heard of. Nottingham is full of strange names, so theirs did not stand out for their strangeness.

Saint Steven and Saint Joan had an elder brother, whose hair around his cock Car could not stop thinking about. His name was Saint Christopher, named after the man who carried the child Christ across a tempestuous river. Car wished Saint Christopher would do the same for him.

The foursome then—Saint Steven, Saint Joan, Corner Pin and Car— decided to form an organisation. It took them the whole of one Saturday to do it. They cut out badges, gave each other ranks and responsibilities, named enemies and allies, decided territories and made a club folder to record the triumphs and failures they would experience together. One unaware ally, because they wanted the organisation to be international, was the Norwegian vicar Corner Pin had mistaken for his father. Saint Joan was in fact slightly older than Car, but agreed that he should become Commander-in-Chief because it all happened in his garden. The others took secondary but equally glorious titles and the organisation was in existence. They thought and argued for hours over a name but eventually decided to call themselves The Shark Club.

The Shark Club came to *mean* Saturdays. It ran wonderfully as an organisation, balancing between fun and war. This balance was maintained because war was fun, and conducted exclusively on two fronts. The first front line was the imaginary sabre-toothed rodent. Its existence was never doubted by The Shark Club and many Saturdays were spent outwitting it and plotting its downfall.

These were dirty days. Gardens are filthy places for children who spend most of their time on the ground stalking strange beasts. A beast more real to the average observer lived next door to Corner Pin and Car, and its name was Mr Black. The second front line. He lived with his wife, whom no-one ever saw, and hated The Shark Club, though he did not know their generic name. To him the Club was a sadistic gift from the devil. They were invaders to be dealt with accordingly. Mr Black's plan of action seemed to consist only of being as horrible as possible to the four children, hoping that this would make them fear him and leave him alone. It was a defensive position. The Club took such a position to be offensive. The worse Mr Black became, the more he inflamed the war. The more they feared him, the more determined they grew in their belief that he wished to destroy them. Everything he did possessed great significance as they spied on him through the tall hedges. If he was digging his garden he would be preparing a trench from which to launch vicious attacks on the Club. If he went anywhere in his car he would soon return with a boot full of supplies and ammunition. If it was hot and he removed his shirt to sunbathe, his reptilian skin would at any moment expand and transform him into a hideous monster. If he did transform he could leap easily over the hedge and rip The Shark Club to pieces. If he shouted at them great lengths of blue flame shot out of his mouth. The fact that his wife was never seen was because he had slowly killed and eaten her.

But violence was not the sole thrust of the Club. There was an element of science, especially from the Commander-in-Chief. Car was, even as a child, in love with the sea. He loved Nottingham but regretted where it sat. He was a true islander, a Briton who loved to stand on his country's coastline, feeling safe and removed, letting the wind push his face. Saint Steven and Saint Joan never came on the family trips over to the Lincolnshire coast, but Corner Pin and Car loved them. The father always drove their rusty Citroen which rose from the ground when the ignition was turned. The mother sat beside him in the front and Corner Pin and Car stared as the East Midlands flashed by outside their windows. On days to the coast everyone got up early. The mother packed a picnic of sandwiches and coffee; no tea because the father did not like its taste, though she did. The father said that one flask was enough for any family. He never wore the collar God had placed around his neck on those trips, because some years before he'd been laughed at by a gang of young men and backed down without saying anything. They would arrive at a beach late morning and stay there until late afternoon before driving back to Nottingham.

Their house on Pierrepont Road had a number of small outhouses, and in one of these Car had what he called a 'shell cupboard'. This was an old free-standing bookshelf, and on it Car displayed all the shells he found over the years of visiting the sea. The shell cupboard stood in a narrow outhouse, empty except for Car's collection, and this place smelt strongly of the sea. There were hundreds of shells on display, but Car especially loved his razor shells. These were long delicate symmetrical objects that he usually found low on the beach, near the water. His favourite was a giant amongst the others, which were all about four inches long. This one measured nine and was brilliant white with thin black stripes. When he was older he held this shell close to his face and thought about times when shells like this were the most important things.

One particular trip to the East Midlands coast remained in his memory. Car had reached the age of about fourteen, with Corner Pin a couple of years behind him. The Shark Club still met but they were all becoming interested in other things. Saint Joan was fifteen and Saint Steven was the same age as Corner Pin, around twelve. The family had driven across Lincolnshire to the sea as usual and set themselves on the sand. It was a very hot summer and a lot of people had come from the oppressive heat of Nottingham, Lincoln, Derby and Leicester to feel the cool wind off the sea. Many of them were almost naked, getting sun into their skin and running through the waves. Car was by this time aware of being aware of male bodies. He found himself repelled by the curves of women, preferring to chronicle the sharp lines of men. And so he found himself watching a man in a cove for the first time.

He had said to the mother and father that he was going for a walk. He had seen a man in his early twenties walking past them wearing only yellow shorts. He had wanted to follow him. He followed him. The man clambered over rocks and hard grass for about half an hour before descending into a tiny cove that no-one else had discovered. There was a miniature beach twenty feet long which dropped suddenly away into waist-high water. For a while the man lay on the beach, oblivious to the fact that he was being watched because Car had followed him silently, as he had trained the others in The Shark Club to do. He watched from behind a rock as the man stood up and sauntered down to the water. Just before wading in, the man pulled down his yellow shorts and was naked. The sun lit parts of him it had not had a chance to brown before. The wind dropped. There was a smell of salt and earth in Car's nose. He did not remove his eyes from the man's body. He understood true muscles, and deep in his brain an acceptance grew that this was the shape he would love. The man went into the water and swam powerfully for a few minutes before walking out of the water to where his shorts lay on the sand. Car saw beautiful black hair he had only heard whispers about and remembered the story of Saint Christopher. On his elated walk back to the mother and father he found a nine inch white razor shell with thin black stripes, and kept it to remind him of when distance was exciting and enough.

The Shark Club began to dehisce as you might expect a heart constructed with sections of other hearts to dehisce. The last meeting of the Club took place behind the compost heap as usual. All four members sat and looked at one another. They had less and less to do as an organisation because Mr Black had moved north of the River Trent and none of them believed that the sabre-toothed rodent existed any longer. Magic had been left behind and replaced by sex. In other words, they were no longer children. Car never told The Shark Club about his investigations into his own attractions because he thought they might regard him as the enemy within. But Saint Steven and Saint Joan were more forthcoming. They had fallen in love with each other. Corner Pin and Car sat and listened as they told of noticing each other's bodies in the bath when they were younger and feeling lost and disappointed when their mother suggested it was time for them to have separate baths. Saint Joan found herself in need of small acts of affection and could find them nowhere else. Saint Steven enjoyed the haven of his sister and each held the other against the world. In later years they were mocked and martyred, stoned and burnt by accusation.

Life continued as church for Corner Pin and Car. The father stood in his pulpit with as much skill as ever. But away from there he was investigating his own attractions. The mother noticed smells on him that had not been there before. They were the smells of other skin.

This was the fourth malady.

She loved her boys more deeply as her husband turned his face away from hers more frequently. She decided to protect them from his neglect by doubling her own attention, so they would not become aware of it. This used an energy she had not thought possible. It was an energy from a well present only in women, and she drew from it increasingly as her boys reached their teens. She had read once of a story of a car crash. A woman was standing in the front window of her house, waiting for her husband to return with their daughter from school. She saw their car turn the corner at the end of the street, but for some reason it was travelling at high speed. Her husband was at the wheel but he lost control. The car hit the kerb and overturned. The woman ran out onto the street screaming her daughter's name, already knowing her husband was dead. The woman looked inside the car and saw that her little girl was trapped. The only way to rescue her would be to lift the car. Petrol was now leaking and the car was on fire. The woman got so angry at her husband's recklessness and at watching her daughter die that she grabbed the car with both hands and flipped it over as if it were a coin. Car's mother tried to rescue them by becoming angry, hiding and protecting them whatever the cost to herself. But tension grew in the house, and the garden could no longer satisfy what Car desired. At the age of eighteen he decided to leave Nottingham and travelled to another city, the city where he first met two other residents of Tigguacobaucc, Hickling Laing and Drury, and where his parents had begun their flying.

A year later Corner Pin, now aged seventeen, began running. He had come home one afternoon and found his mother standing in the kitchen with a white unopened envelope in her hand. He could see that she knew what it contained, and she asked him to phone one of the church elders. He phoned one who was a good friend of the family called Coe, who came over to the house immediately. All three sat in the living room of the house and the mother opened the letter, which had nothing written on the envelope. It was a letter from the father to the mother saying that he had suffered and had made her suffer and had left.

This was a Monday. Only the day before, the father had stood in his pulpit proclaiming the sanctity of marriage. Corner Pin watched his mother cry, and cried himself. He had never had a father who held him and whispered special things in his ear, but he knew also that any chance of that ever happening was now gone. The father had not said much in his letter, except that he had gone to the south coast with the woman whose skin Corner Pin's mother had begun to smell on her husband's skin. He would not be coming back to Nottingham. Car was telephoned of course, and came to his city for a while but there was little he could do and went back to the flat he shared with Hickling Laing and Drury in Birmingham.

Corner Pin began to run. To begin with, he ran within himself. His nightmares as a child had, as he learned to expect, come true. The rhythm of uncertainty jumped out of his dreams and into his life. His first reaction was to cover his head with his hands and curl away. But he was not still in his head. He found himself running like a mad thing around what had happened. His father's letter chased him like a ferocious dog, biting his heels at every chance. The man who made him feel safe, as he watched the light pour onto him through church windows, had flung himself from under the light into the darkness. Corner Pin could not picture what he looked like. He realised for the first time that he had never known his father because he could not remember him. He had many memories of being with him, of the father driving them all to the sea, or calling him and Car in from the garden. He knew he must have sat hundreds of times eating with him but did not know how his father ate. He saw clearly now how the mother had protected him and his brother from what he would not call, by turning turbulence into, poetry.

His father's dissension from the church affected his own belief in God. It became stronger and more private. He could not face the familiar faces at what had once been his father's church because, just as they had always asked him how school was going, they now asked him if he was alright, if he was coping. He did not have an answer to these questions. Corner Pin was amazed at the dry canyon left by someone who had hardly been there in the first place, but like his childhood nightmares, he was more terrified of the absence than the absentee.

What surprised him and his mother was that he did not turn to her for comfort. He retired from family life and searched himself. Though only young, he became deeply involved with himself, and grew sadder each day. Sadness he believed to be the correct tower from which to view himself, but he was always forced to climb higher as his view was constantly obscured by clouds.

And the size of things is what youth is all about.

Car's approach to loss was to reach new heights of gregarity. He opened his mind and ushered everyone he could reach inside, where they were welcomed as saviours. Car dispensed with God. Although God had undoubtedly answered Car's requests to find himself in the company of men who loved the company of their own kind, he had slowly found that he was capable of attracting them himself. He understood that being nineteen was its own deity. Car was busy anyway, learning that medical information can make the person providing it important.

Corner Pin attempted to turn the world into an imaginary place, a place where nothing mattered except his own feelings and the understanding of them. Materialism came to mean more to him than simply the acquisition of goods and wealth. Materialism was the epitome of reality, of tangibility, and so Corner Pin detested it. He began to construct a world where real people mixed freely with those he imagined. In the corridors of his mind ghosts and angels jostled for space with people he knew and had met in the material world. In this place of imaginary beings God was easy to see. God would not, could not, leave a place that didn't exist. For a time, Corner Pin found in himself a feeling of security and the nightmares stopped.

Watching him from outside, his mother felt as though all had left her. The father had gone to live by the sea, Car was in Birmingham and Corner Pin had curled tightly away from her. She was lost and lonely for two years. Slowly, though, the mother began to enjoy herself. In her own way she had been formidable all her life, but this passion had been crushed and contained, caged for years by her husband. He had believed it incorrect for women to speak, and planted her out of sight in the kitchen. But this was over. The mother saw how Car was dealing with loss and decided to follow her son's example. She developed skills she'd not used since being a teenager. She became reckless and, though nearly fifty, climbed the faces of cliffs, pulling her body as high as it could go, forcing herself to see the world from a great height.

Her trips to the Peak District were a corrigendum to her life until this point. She would pull out of Nottingham early on a Saturday and would then sit on the train to Sheffield. They would board a bus and drive through the grey city into the hills, where they and the wind enjoyed each other's company. This became a regular journey, but one particular journey changed the mother's life. She fell in love with a millionaire on top of a mountain.

Despite this happiness, for Corner Pin it was the fifth malady.

By that time Corner Pin had begun to run through the streets at night. The pain in his legs he had suffered since childhood had prepared him for this. No pain could stop him or even slow him down. He gathered speed from about the age of twenty until he became a blur at the age of twenty-three. From the beginning he only ran at night, under cover of the darkness that made parts of Nottingham a warren. The most common route for Corner Pin was to travel north through the city. He would race across Trent Bridge and up London Road to the Lace Market, but instead of turning into it, would continue up Hollow Stone and Bellar Gate and past Plumtre Street. Then he turned towards Huntingdon Street and onto Mansfield Road.

At the top of the hill a large cemetery begins and sweeps down the other side of the hill. Corner Pin was not yet aware of Tigguacobaucc, the city of sand beneath Nottingham, but it was up here that he eventually noticed Tigguacobaucc surfacing through the graves. Tombstones in the Rock Cemetery stand between low stumps of bedrock sandstone, all that remains of the pillars which supported the roof of the old sand mine before its collapse and destruction in the early years of the nineteenth century. Most of these caves are clearly visible from the surface and are the various old quarries, sand mines, collapsed mines and catacombs in and around the cemetery. Corner Pin paused in the Rock Cemetery one night and saw these dead caves on the surface. He began to wonder about all the stories he had heard of a city under his own.

Usually he would run through the Rock Cemetery and into The Forest, a rectangle the size of a small village with one side that runs up to the cemetery. This side is covered in trees and is a favourite place for people to pay to hold one another. The largest part of The Forest is not a forest but a vast area of playing fields. Running the full length between the hill of trees and the flat recreation area is a wide path of pink stones. The path is lit from one end to the other by an austere row of tall lamps that flood the pink path in orange light. The Forest is known to everyone in Nottingham because it becomes Goose Fair in October, transforming the rectangle into the largest European carpet of lights. Corner Pin travels too fast through The Forest to notice many things, but he could swear he once saw his brother wrapped in someone else amongst the trees.

After The Forest, Corner Pin would run up Noel Street and onto Mount Hooton Road before turning off it and through Waterloo Promenade. This is a pedestrian strip, banked on each side of the path by grass. Rows of large Victorian terraces stand behind ornate black iron fencing on both sides and Corner Pin, despite his disillusionment and hatred for materialism, loved these houses and the wealth they held. Then his legs would carry him the short way up Waterloo Road, over Southey Street and along Forest Road West on to Forest Road East. He would rush past the prostitutes angling by the kerb and back down Mansfield Road towards Trent Bridge.

Corner Pin ran across Nottingham like this for months before needing more security. But he received a letter from his father one morning which sent him underground. The letter was written on a large piece of white paper, just as the father's leaving note had been. There were very few words however, and most of them conjured a sad picture. Corner Pin and Car and the mother knew that the father was not alone, that he lived with the woman whose skin had alerted the mother to impending shock. But in his letter the father decided to throw himself on a canvas of loneliness and regret.

The letter began with love. The father said things to Corner Pin that his son had until then only ever heard from the pulpit. The father wrote: *"I love my children. I am proud of my boys. I would die for them."* And Corner Pin read these words and did not know what they meant; they were as distant as when he had heard them announced to a congregation from the pulpit. But they were not ineffective. Corner Pin found his father's voice louder than all others in the bustling corridors of his mind. The ghosts of past figures and the angels of Corner Pin's fervent belief were all talking at once, but above them all was his father's voice, insistent in regret. His was the voice of reality.

The father did not write to Corner Pin about God; it was the first time Corner Pin had been spoken to by his father without that shadow the size of the universe standing between them. But God had not followed the father away from Nottingham. He had been discarded with the collar and the father had made himself free.

Corner Pin's father relaxed in a way he had not thought possible, or at least not possible for him. The world had become intelligible and he delighted in it. He had once deliberately thrown away subjects that could be pinned down and decided to exchange the spanner for the pulpit, fiddling instead with the mysterious workings of God. These mysteries became swirling colours, ever-changing and indistinguishable. He had laughed at attempts to classify the earth by numbers or formulæ, finding such efforts misguided and pointless. The father revelled in the arrogance that accompanies those who believe they can know the world without understanding it. He believed that his lack of evidence for his faith made that faith stronger, and mocked those who required proof before acceptance. But the energy needed to maintain an assailable position had given him no rest, no peace, and his natural need for these two things eventually became his highest priority. In his new house by the sea, he threw away childish acceptance and became a questioning man. His garden was his laboratory and his plants experiments. But he grew no fruit. This garden was many times smaller than the one he had left in Nottingham. It could bear him no raspberries under a green marquee, nor produce apples from old trees. Instead of harvesting and thanking God for his goodness he learned to fill the garden with flowers. They were of no use. They could not be eaten. They appeared only for a short time. They required a higher level of patience. He grew them only for the sake of their beauty, and so he stumbled upon the reason for the existence of the earth—that there was no reason for its existence.

But in the words he sent to Corner Pin the father mentioned none of this. In a single paragraph he had disturbed Corner Pin enough to force him into the caves, into Tigguacobaucc. The father said that every night was the same. Every night he took himself down to the sea and walked along the coast road through his new home town of Hastings. Every night the rain would seep through his coat. Every night he would stand under great waves that momentarily escaped from the sea and towered over the road before crashing over the path and the father and returning to their tumultuous home. The father was being drenched by regret. That Corner Pin could not be sure if this was true did not matter, though he remembered his father to be an habitual liar. But lies were frippery to Corner Pin. They could not hold him in their grip because he was too fast for them. And he was getting faster.

This was the sixth malady.

It was on one of his runs to The Forest and back that Corner Pin first came across the entrance to the Peel Street Caves. He stopped and pushed the door open, then carefully went down the steps that took him ten metres under Nottingham. He had discovered a place to run without being disturbed, a new hiding place, a new silent place for thoughts to run, a new dark place for bodies to slide against other bodies. He began to live here.

In Tigguacobaucc he was not alone of course, though the city of sand is big enough to please a lost young man of twenty-three who wishes to rush through its pillars and arches without being questioned. Corner Pin no longer writes poetry, but he has given me the last poem he wrote before diving underground with the rest of us.

Triangle Trick by Corner Pin

What happened has made me
a last resting place for questions
that are not my own.
THE FAMOUS TRIANGLE TRICK,
appearing from my parents like magic
in a quick flick of their wrists,
a puff of intimacy.

The act has finished now though
and our triangle is north to south,
points propelled apart
like spit from the mouths
of one another,
flung further than possible.
It's left to me to absorb the questions;
How's your mother?
Is your father alone still,
by the sea?
Listening to them tug until
they break the rules of geometry.
Me, the sole part of the show
that failed to vanish,
my body
their best trick yet.

Corner Pin runs only at night. He rarely runs on Nottingham's surface, preferring the life underground. But during the day he rests his legs, the legs that as a child had hinted to him what his life would become. Fear has been replaced by sadness, and Corner Pin has been hurt more than any of us. His story is sad, but like all sad stories has importance lying within it.

He thinks of his family often, especially Car, who he heard has returned to Nottingham. He is certain they could not recognise one another. At least Car could not see his younger brother under the painful skin of Corner Pin's face. A pain of exertion and sadness. A lost face running at high speed through the underground world of Tigguacobaucc. And perhaps too, Corner Pin could not pick his elder brother out from all who come down to the caves, for Car has returned to Nottingham without his name. He arrived here heavily under the weight of The Rings. He finds it hard to trust himself because so many people have said they cannot trust him. Car's Rings grow more complex when he can hear those voices clearly but is not sure if he should trust them.

A city of two parts. There is a rumour that Car has been given a replacement name. That Nottingham has welcomed its prodigal son. A city of two parts. An invention and a truth.

Corner Pin has met many people down here, around these pillars. He is surrounded beneath this famous city by others who have all come to shelter or rejoice. Although he finds it hard to trust them, he does speak to them when he is resting during the day. One person he has spoken to is called Old Angel, the person who suggested I tell you the stories of these people. Though he does not tell stories himself, he is a reader of books and understands that stories can free those who tell them and those who listen. My name is Tigguacobaucc and I am trying to be freed.

This is the seventh malady.

Old Angel listened carefully to what Corner Pin had to say. His ears were pinned to their head with tales of the garden and of The Shark Club. He sympathised with Corner Pin's premonitory legs and how they told him of the life to come. He recognised their ability to see into the future because he too believed in visions. The vision that had once come to him was of the city of sand being filled with concrete, covering us cowering within it. I do not think that this will ever happen, but I have been wrong about many things. Corner Pin told Old Angel everything and Old Angel answered. Old Angel never became the most important part of Corner Pin's life, as he did mine, but in some ways he saved him as he saved me.

Old Angel gave Corner Pin a book. Corner Pin had told of the fruit his family used to grow in their long garden, how there were raspberries and apples. Old Angel took this memory to mean that Corner Pin had opinions on fruit and recommended a book by a well-known lover of fruit. Corner Pin read the book while his legs rested. He read it with his back against the sandy walls of Tigguacobaucc. All his life, Corner Pin had believed demons to be evil. He thought they lived where God could never live and so did not want anything to do with them. Though curled up within himself or running unaware of others, he had made space for hatred. He interpreted what had happened to his family as part of the constant battle between angels and demons, the war that members of his father's old church did not like to discuss, even though they believed in it. But here was a book that talked openly about the war and did not take sides. The book said that love could exist in beings who were evil just as it existed in those who were good. He thought of his father and the hurt he had caused. He pictured his father walking along the face of the sea, under the huge curling arms of the waves. And he thought of the garden in which he and Car had grown up. And he remembered the summer light striking it. And he thought he could hear in his head the distant sound of the mother praying for it all to end.

And the size of things is what youth is all about.

And then he saw the mother kissing her millionaire on a mountain. And he saw the father relaxed, with the top button of his shirt joyfully open, lying in the arms of the woman with strong smelling skin. And he saw Car, lost and without a name but with friends. And he saw himself running underground, far beneath Nottingham, like a mad thing. And Corner Pin's voice grew louder and he started to call out. He screamed the scream that would wake him when he was a child. He lifted his mouth and pointed the sound upwards, made it bore through the sandstone up to the street and pushed it into the air above the city. He willed it to echo over Nottingham, and as he shouted for help the busy corridors of his mind shook and the ghosts and angels began to run for cover. They dived out of his ears and scuttled to safety in the darkness of the caves. They fell from his nose. They jumped on the stretches of sound from his mouth and rode the sound into the air of the city. In the rush to escape they trampled Corner Pin's faith in God, and God jumped on the last scream, ducking between Corner Pin's teeth and vanishing in the vaulted labyrinth.

God had abandoned him because God knew he was calling a gentle demon. With his head clear of faith and restless memories, Corner Pin had silence. There was nothing moving inside him except his heart, which he had held tight should it have been tugged away by the exodus. He had not lost his heart. He turned his ears to the stairs that led up to Peel Street and listened. For many minutes there was nothing, only the distant sound of Nottingham living the night. But then he picked a strange sound out, faint though getting stronger. It was the sound of beating wings, small and determined.

chapter 4

the story of
hickling laing and drury

HICKLING Laing was born under a sun rising, and as when I was born, this sun rose over Nottingham. These two births occurred on the same day. Hickling Laing is close to me because he began in this city but left for a while, and he left but returned to become stuck with loving this one. My name is Tigguacobaucc and my story could easily be told through the story of Hickling Laing and his imaginary friend, Drury. It's time to let that happen.

A city of two parts. An invention and a truth.

Until now, all the stories of my friends have taken place south of Trent Bridge, but Hickling Laing arrived from between his mother's legs on Mapperley Top, north of the famous river. Let me take you there. The County of Nottinghamshire is as flat as it has always been, but these days the land is joined to the sky by towering power stations, thrown up from the fields as if built by the movements of tectonic plates. The great grey tubes are not everywhere but they can be seen from everywhere. They run power into Nottingham, which is not flat. The city rises and falls independent of its county, echoing its history. As it travels out from the centre and further from the caves it pulls itself over hills and into the miniature valleys. Nottingham has flooded areas that were once the King's own hunting grounds, that once stood as Sherwood Forest. But this growth is not a disaster, for Nottingham has an energy and beauty the forest could never have, and has created new hiding places for outlaws.

Let me take you up from the centre, climbing a vein from the city to the suburbs called Woodborough Road. The north is steeper than the south. Walk with me past gradually larger houses, and on the left is the wealth of Mapperley Park, tree-lined and red-bricked ornate. There is nothing to fear though; the gardens are large but there are no lions. We will come face to face with them in another story, another garden. So round Woodborough Road and over the junction onto Plains Road and we are walking across Mapperley Top. From its name you can guess that this place was once merely a hill, but the city has overwhelmed it with shops and houses. Like all big cities, Nottingham is jigsawed by villages slotted together to make one place. Mapperley is one village, surrounded by other parts of the city and juggling its own history with its own futures. Like an arched backbone, the Top rides over this area, a spine of florists and bakeries, takeaways and banks. And it was into this piece of the puzzle that Hickling Laing fell from between his mother's legs.

Hickling Laing's mother had met his father only once, and decided that once would be enough. She preferred the company of women, and although she was happy to give birth to a boy, she did not relish the thought of what he would become. There was no malice in her, though; she did not hate men, merely their muscles and hair. Women gave her the endless smooth limbs that she enjoyed owning herself. Hickling Laing fell from a woman called Coronation, and Coronation fell for the midwife who caught him, called Hazel Grove.

Coronation watched exhausted, as Hazel Grove cleared the blood that Hickling Laing had drawn out with him, and fell in love with her. She held the baby close to her body, but did not give him her attention. She only had eyes for Hazel Grove and so could not meet the remarkable eyes of her son, looking into her, black as coal. Hickling Laing was born with disbelief in his eyes. He was never blind to the workings of the human heart, because at home he saw it tick and grind in front of him. He saw love but did not feel it. This would later become his passport to Tigguacobaucc, an underground shelter for the ignored. Hickling Laing grew up on his own. Just as his mother preferred her own limbs, he would sing to himself. As she liked to run her fingers along the familiar, he conversed with few other than his own voice. He would tell himself stories, and become in one way a singer; and the diapason of his voice has been called astounding, but also a frustration. Hickling Laing could never quite decide at what pitch to tell stories. This is not to say that he was unhappy.

Mapperley Top was a good place for a boy who liked his own company to grow up. As a teenager, Hickling Laing suffered no angst. He did not undergo Corner Pin's strict religious childhood, and he had not lost his heart as Black Boy had lost his. He lived in a lonely world but was happy there. Born and grown on Mapperley Top, he had two favourite places to sit with himself. Sweeping down from the Top into Sherwood is Woodthorpe Drive. From the Mapperley end there is a view across all of north-west Nottingham, and Hickling Laing would stand there and think about his city. He would consider his options, wondering if Nottingham really was the place in which he could be happiest. He looked over his home town and saw it through his black eyes. He was not loved at home. When he was young and standing like this with Nottingham as far as the eye could see, he made the mistake of believing that because he was not loved then he could not love, and if he was unable to love somewhere then he could not lose it. This logic both drove him away and returned him.

Further down winding Woodthorpe Drive is Woodthorpe Grange Park. Compared to the many other green areas of the city this is a small stretch, but Hickling Laing liked being there. Within the grounds of the park there are sunken gardens, where Hickling Laing would sit and think. This was his second favourite place. Down here amongst the plants, Hickling Laing met Drury for the first time. It happened on Hickling Laing's eighteenth birthday, which of course was also mine, though we were unaware of one another back then. Drury came to Hickling Laing as Orange Boy did to others. He appeared like a wisp. Drury's appearance coincided with Hickling Laing wishing him to appear, and so from the very beginning he was imaginary.

Hickling Laing was born with disbelief in his eyes. The fact that one of his wishes had come true did not affect this birthright. He had heard of stranger things than the sudden appearance of a friend happening in Nottingham, and so accepted Drury merely as a symptom of living here.

Drury, like many wishes, turned out to be the opposite of what Hickling Laing had wanted. Instead of providing a keen ear for Hickling Laing's flourishing atheism, he argued the case for the defence. Drury believed in God. After a few months of living in Nottingham he understood that the church has no grip on this place, though there is the rag-and-bone bric-a-brac selection of ways to worship Whatever. But he discovered that God, however he is painted, is no clarion here. Drury became sad at the decline of God, but as he is imaginary himself he is to be expected to relate to his own kind. Hickling Laing grew to hate God more than anyone in Tigguacobaucc, but both he and Drury, like all truly content beings, merely enjoyed their sparring. Hearing another opinion did not dislodge them from their own, nor did it make them unhappy. They each came to love the other for listening.

As he moved through his late teens, Hickling Laing saw less and less of his mother. This did not disturb him, as she had never given him her attention anyway. At this time he still lived with her on Mapperley Top, but they only crossed on the stairs. Hickling Laing spent most of his time walking down Woodborough Road into the city, or looking at himself in mirrors. Like Black Boy, he found mirrors to be a comfort and a motivation. Like Black Boy, he had no money with which to buy them. Unlike Black Boy, he did not possess looks good enough to force women simply to hand over their mirrors to him. He did not have a large collection. But the one or two he hung in his room were enough to encourage confidence. Hickling Laing would sit and look at his features before leaving the house: brown hair, wide eyebrows, large nose, jet black jet eyes. Physically he is scrawny with a little elegance. He is neither a delight nor a terror to look at.

Hickling Laing learned to delight in terror. After spending years at his mother's house he managed to rent a small flat above a shop that sold everything. This flat was suitable for his needs, which were few but epic. He took it so he could be free to plan courses of action. Hickling Laing's mother paid for all of this. She had not looked into his eyes as a baby, but she had held him, and there was no malice in her emotional neglect. It was just that he had become a young man, and so automatically failed to interest her in any way. She was not without guilt though, and gave him an allowance to live on, as much to get him out of her sight as to expand his own.

The shop was not far from his mother's house anyway, and Hickling Laing drew his breath when he first looked from the window in the back room. Through the glass was the view of north-west Nottingham he had loved for so long. He looked out of this window and decided to take the flat that went with it. Hickling Laing now lived on Greengate Avenue just around the corner from Mapperley Top. The flat consisted of a front room, where Hickling Laing put a couple of comfortable chairs and where Drury slept; a bathroom; a yellowing kitchen;

and the wonderful back room, where he slept himself. Across from his bed, Hickling Laing had placed a big old desk and covered it with his collection of newspaper clippings. He also bought piles of blank sheets of paper. There was no television, only candles to stare into and think. A person whose wishes come true has no real need of television.

A person with no story is a diseased person. As is a person with too many.

A person with few needs can be happy very quickly. Hickling Laing fell head-long into this category, but he was then left with a great deal of time on his hands. To fill it he would go into the city, and to go there meant passing people who disgusted him. These people would stand in the city centre offering leaflets to all who took them and all who wouldn't. They are also responsible for much of the story of Hickling Laing and Drury, though they would hate to think so.

Sticks and stones. Sticks and stones may break my bones. My name is Tigguacobaucc. A replacement name in a city of two parts. Inventions and truths are driving me forward and I have been told that by telling stories I will remem-ber my own story. I have been warned that the caves under my famous city could one day be bloated with concrete, though I do not believe this will hap-pen. If I believe strongly enough then indeed this might be averted. Nottingham has welcomed me as it has welcomed you, but in return it cries for rescue. The city will not trick you as its inhabitants might, but it is as scared as they are. The city does not want to become one of the many lost that it shelters—it fears becoming a casualty by association. My name is Tigguacobaucc and I am safe here, but confused. My mind is a conglomerate, a meeting of many others who do not understand the nature of The Rings any more than I do. The Rings are manifested differently in each of us, preying on points of weakness like a man-tis, prying into us, setting us into a spin. My Rings are terrible: they have blanked me, blanketed me with the stories of others. If I tell each story, each layer that covers me, I will bare myself and remember. My name is Tigguacobaucc but it is not my name. I want back the name I cannot remember, the name that can pull me from The Rings, the name that can never hurt me.

Hickling Laing ran his black eyes up the body of an old man who stood across from him on Albert Street. This was Saturday afternoon and the city heaved. The man was shouting from what he claimed to be the vantage point of heaven. Nottingham was not listening to him, but Hickling Laing was, and Drury stood embarrassed beside him. They had come to town specifically to find people like this. It was part of Hickling Laing's plan of action, and he heard every word the man shouted at the crowd. The man wore a very brown big coat and with it, a bright red baseball cap. No one listened but everyone looked. He had at his feet a battered briefcase open on the ground which overflowed with promotional literature. At the top of his voice he claimed to be a door-to-door salesman, selling God without incurring any cost except the heart. Hickling Laing had no personal experience of people like this so he decided to research. He walked over to the man, bent down, and lifted a tightly folded piece of yellow paper, putting it in his pocket and moving away. The man looked at him and Hickling Laing looked back, searing into the man's heart with his vacuous eyes. There was no more shouting. The man could not release himself from the grip of Hickling Laing's immovable disbelief and as he stared, his skin began to visibly tighten around his mouth. All afternoon he had raised his voice with a face set stern in the judgment of God. He had been screaming happiness from a mouth deep in his rock face, and there was no movement. He talked of terrible consequences, of the wages of this thing he called sin. He scared children and moved people away from him because he appeared to them to be the very face of madness. And deep inside, he saw himself doing this to these people. He knew that he was in some ways attacking them, harming them, disturbing them, and he wished he could stop. But he could not. God was a powerful drug surging through his veins. The drug awoke him early on Saturday mornings and lifted him clean out of his bed. It dragged clothes over his body and made him eat breakfast. He wanted to be still sleeping but he was unable to sleep. The drug pulled the front door of his little house shut behind him and walked him to the bus stop. It stepped him onto the bus and handed over a fare. It jumped his body off at the city centre and stood him on Albert Street, where it seemed to know there would be many people. Finally, it opened a briefcase crammed with leaflets on the pavement and forced his mouth wide, releasing terrible words that scared children. But this Saturday was different. A young man with eyes as strong as the drug was looking at him, into him, fighting him. He could not pull away. Even the drug could not jolt him from the stare of Hickling Laing, whose eyes drew him in like black holes, ineffable in their depth. The man found himself with one arm stretching towards Hickling Laing, reaching for the joy that he could feel from the darkness of disbelief, and the other arm being gripped by the drug, by God. The man was being torn between a place where God could not exist and the withdrawal of leaving a place where he pumped through the blood like a chemical, alien to his body. The ligature that God had performed on the man was strong, but not under the eyes of Hickling Laing. The bindings that held the man's heart close to God came loose under the strain and broke. He felt himself propelled towards the darkness, away from the light, and into a safe place, a place where Hickling Laing was happy and where he now discovered he could make others happy too.

What the people of Albert Street saw was a crazy man, whom they knew well from their Saturday afternoons in town, staring into a young man's eyes and being quietened by them. They watched as he walked away from his briefcase full of bright evil words. They could not see the battle that had freed him from addiction, from God, but they saw the skin around his mouth tighten into a smile. Quiet. They also watched as small tears ran over the smile. They had witnessed Hickling Laing converting his first Christian.

The two men—one old, one young, both free—did not speak. Hickling Laing took a bus back up Woodborough Road to Mapperley Top, and he and Drury sat down in the back room overlooking Nottingham. Hickling Laing pulled out the yellow leaflet from his pocket and began to read what it said. He needed to know the lines where battle had been drawn. He must harness his eyes and direct them where their gaze would be most effective, and to do that he must understand belief. The leaflet had a section which explained what it called the 'Doctrinal Basis' upon which its view of the world was founded. Drury listened as Hickling Laing read these statements to him.

The Father, Son and Holy Spirit, these three being one God.

The sovereignty of God in creation, revelation, redemption and final judgment.

The incarnation, death, resurrection, ascension and future return of Jesus Christ, the divine Son of God.

The sinfulness of human nature since the fall, and the necessity for repentance towards God and faith in Jesus Christ.

The forgiveness of sins through the sacrificial death of Jesus Christ on our behalf.

The work of the Holy Spirit in granting repentance and faith, and also in indwelling and sanctifying the individual believer.

The one holy catholic Church in heaven and earth, which is the Body of Christ and to which all true believers belong.

The divine inspiration and complete trustworthiness of Holy Scripture as originally given, and its supreme authority in all matters of faith and conduct.

In becoming a Member of the Fellowship of God, I declare my faith in Jesus Christ as my Saviour, my Lord and my God whose atoning sacrifice is the only and all-sufficient ground of my salvation. I will seek both in life and thought to be ruled by the teaching of the Bible, believing it to be the inspired Word of God.

Hickling Laing finished reading and looked at Drury, who was smiling. They talked late into the night as they usually did, before Drury returned to the front room and rested by vanishing into thin air.

Hickling Laing used the night to continue his research into the elements of belief. His large collection of newspaper cuttings were all concerned with faith and its effects on human beings. Most articles were from right-wing papers, whose editors seemed to be under the impression that if their papers were peppered with God then more people would read them. This was of course, for the most part, true. But at the same time, Hickling Laing noticed they were not religious tracts. God was used particularly on the issue of nationhood. Britain could always be sure that God would follow her soldiers into the danger zones of the world. Britain and America were convinced that God was on their side. This enabled these two countries to trample any other that did not view God in exactly the same way. They called this process 'protecting our freedoms.' Hickling Laing knew that his eyes could free those held in God. He did not believe their belief and destroyed it with incredulity. From the moment he fell from between his mother's legs he had been unable to equate superstition and faith with freedom. He also wondered about the 'freedoms' of the naked girls draped beside these articles on God. His black eyes stared down the bodies of these girls, and his own body did not dream but shook.

But it was not simply the mad papers that were infected with the presence of God. Hickling Laing also had many cuttings from wider papers made with longer words. These papers attempted to keep their distance from God while acknowledging him. Hickling Laing knew this to be futile. He remembered the strength it had taken to pull the loud old man away from the grip of God, and understood that if God is recognised at all, then people become trapped. These larger papers treated Britain as a laboratory; they performed experiments on it. They would commission research into what they called *The Spiritual Health of*

Britain or something similar. Hickling Laing frequently grew nauseous when reading these reports. What shocked him severely was that most British people tested under laboratory conditions proclaimed some kind of belief in God, while at the same time claiming not to have given the matter much thought. Hickling Laing could not grasp how people came to conclusions of such magnitude, however vague, without consideration. Once experiments were completed on the damask of the British nation, the papers would bring their findings back to their spotless offices and dissect the information. Pronouncements would follow, often in the weekend editions, and readers would be made to feel safe in the knowledge that Britain still feared God.

That Saturday morning, before going into the city and rescuing an old man, Hickling Laing had visited one of his favourite shops on Woodborough Road. Just at the bend where Woodborough turns into Plains there is a shop selling used furniture. The furniture is too good to be junk and too cheap to be antique, making it all within reach and desirable to Hickling Laing. He knew the owner of the shop quite well and liked him because he once heard the man say to someone that he would never advertise local church theatre productions in his window. Hickling Laing liked bits of furniture, and though he did not have a great deal of money he had been saving for one particular piece. That morning he'd gone into the shop and paid forty pounds for a red leather armchair. It was low to the ground but had high wooden arms that made it perfect for reading. When Hickling Laing sat in it, he rested his elbows on these arms and a book or newspaper clipping would be at exactly the right height. When he'd carried the chair back to the flat he placed it facing the window in his room. And this was where he sat that evening, thinking of the depth of his eyes and the shallowness of newspapers. His new chair was so comfortable that he fell asleep in it, covered in journalistic experiments on Britain.

If you were to own a house on a hill in Nottingham, and awoke one morning to the bright sun, something would be missing. You would stand in large bay windows, searching the early mist and trees for what might be expected. You would spot one or two; they are not extinct. But it is not the familiar skyline of an aged English city. There are hardly any steeples.

This is the scene Hickling Laing looked on the next morning. His window was commanding. He eased himself from the red chair and transferred to the bathroom. This room was entirely white, the colour amidst which Hickling Laing liked to look at himself. There was of course a large mirror in here, and he would stand naked in front of it, staring through black eyes at his long body. His limbs were thin but he moved them well. He knew that someone out there in the city was sure to find him attractive, but he had never had any desire to test this intuition. He was an evangelical, a missionary to Nottingham from a world that so far was populated with very few other than himself. He felt alien but content. A dog in a world of sheep.

He turned the shower on and let the water run across the back of his hand. The temperature was correct and he stepped in. Hickling Laing loved soap and he had lined many kinds along the shelf attached to the wall beneath the shower head. The first real decision of the day was to choose which soap to use. They were of many colours and possessed the fragrances of many fruits. His most frequent choice was a bright orange bar, whose smell would flare into the nose. Oranges. He picked their scent from the shelf and ran it over his skin. The water was very warm and he began to think. The first thing that entered his head was Drury, who immediately appeared in the bathroom and stood watching Hickling Laing shower. He heard Drury speak through the water, switched the shower off and stepped out into a towel. They had become very close since Hickling Laing had first wished for a companion, and he was used to Drury being with him when he was naked. Like religious experience, Hickling Laing had never had personal contact with men who find the bodies of men attractive, who might find his own body attractive. He knew that those particular rules of attraction were common but held no interest in them himself. He did notice that Drury watched his body carefully. Passion rises in the imaginary as firmly as in the imagination.

Hickling Laing went back to his back room and dressed in the clothes that kept him happy. These were: a pair of blue jeans, a pair of shiny brown shoes, a baggy white shirt and one of his selection of plain waistcoats. This time he pulled his arms through a dark blue one with a gold back-piece.

He rarely ate a lot of breakfast, just cereal he trusted to clear his gut. Coffee was his major drink and he made a cup, drinking it right down before walking round the corner to the local newsagent to buy all the Sunday newspapers. Newspapers, aside from rent, food and bits of furniture, were his biggest outgoing. But they had to be read for purposes of research. Hickling Laing needed to know the world before he could properly attempt to change it. So he and Drury spent most of the day reading the papers and making cuttings of anything remotely involving God. During this early stage of his career as an evangelist, scissors were Hickling Laing's most treasured possession.

My name is Tigguacobaucc and I have made a career from pungence. I am a librarian, surrounded with musty walls and objects. Corners are my breathing spaces. Caves and libraries are my stereophonics. I will guide you through the stories of my friends as I will also guide you around Nottingham. The north is steeper than the south. Lost in the wiles of the walkie-talkie world I have found the place where I am happiest, even though I am not happy. And you are here to see the blink of an eye and things changing in it. You are with us under The Rings, following us along the Trent, over the bridge, within the grace of Lace Market. You have stepped ten metres underground into a city of sand, great passages and arching rooms held by wide pillars. The galleries for our work, shelters for our weaknesses, chambers in which to rejoice and remember. Remember. Recall. Picture. Rediscover. Yaw. And that is what I am here for. Sunken thoughts dredged by the present. What city is this? Nottingham. Why is it famous? For many reasons. What does it hide? Stories. And beneath those? A story. Exaggeration comes in many forms and in all of them it is an under-rated virtue. I will cultivate to reap what I have lost. I will hold my attention and classify all this. File for easy retrieval. Order it. Take advice and listen to the whispers of a demon. Look at them all sitting there in the sand, surrounding you with stories. You devils. Who are we? A genuine mish-mash.

There are too many maladies to count. But the air is clearing around them.

Hickling Laing passed time in personal development, for it was not only in newspapers that designs were made of God. Books handed information over to him too. He began to visit the main library in Nottingham, on Angel Row. On the first few visits he was not a skilled library user. He typed requests into the computer catalogue inefficiently for many weeks before asking those staffing the place to help. But it was in Nottingham that he first discovered the true role and skill of professional librarians. Hickling Laing found their help addictive. He followed them as they searched for answers to his questions, he watched as the library responded to palpation, as they examined it for knowledge. He took books back to the red leather chair and read the night, hardly able to wait for the next visit to the library, the next book. It was in another city though, it would be in Birmingham, that the aid of a librarian would become complicity.

He walked the aisles, books rising past his shoulders. Here in these thin spaces he learnt many things. For months he restricted his mind to fiction, understanding that in invention, truth is often to be found. And the truth for which he scanned stories suffered great stress under those black eyes. He could only be moved, taught, by exceptional books. They needed strong bindings and tight words to withstand the intense glare while he read them. Over time, many found themselves cast to the floor like bad seed; but others, the minority, grew in the environment Hickling Laing provided for them. These books were rarely read by someone who could give the attention that Hickling Laing shone into them. Though books are inanimate, under the correct conditions they have life. Like libraries, they will respond to palpation. It requires only the electricity running from the fingers of a sensitive reader to restart the phloem that was once their constitution.

During the time Hickling Laing was taking to read books, Drury rarely heard from him. He would only appear when thoughts of him entered Hickling Laing's head, and that head was staring at words. Because Hickling Laing, born disbelieving, could not picture God, he did not realise that imaginary beings may not need him. He believed in Drury because his black eyes saw him. Drury lived a life other than when Hickling Laing thought about him. He always came when summoned but this was not resurrection. Drury never died. He found these things difficult to explain to Hickling Laing, so he left them out of their relationship. Through the experience of his own life then, Drury knew that God existed; he could not deny it. They were too alike.

In the spaces where Hickling Laing did not call him, Drury wandered around Nottingham. He was never bored because he had an active mind. Sometimes he visited the few churches in the city, and often appeared in Lincoln, where his favourite cathedral in the East Midlands perched on a high hill overlooking its shire. But Nottingham was usually enough for him. Invisible, he drank in one particular pub called 'The Trip to Jerusalem', and he drank there because he approved of the name. This is the oldest inn in England and is cut from the sandstone hill upon which Nottingham Castle sits. The ceilings are low and the floors flagged. It is a place where history smells, where that most abstract sense is banqueted by the air between the sandy walls. 'The Trip' is a surface level cave, a series of hacked rooms begun in the twelfth century. To sit there with a pint is to kiss Nottingham when it was young. Drury would stand at the old bar listening to ideas on the best way for Nottingham Forest to get back to the Premier League. He heard discussions of English politics, why every party wanted to hold the centre ground, why no-one wished to appear extreme. Why no-one wished. He was always most interested in talk of God, which, for people who lived in a secular city, occurred more than he expected. Drury thought there was a naïve understanding by most that God had ceased to be important mainly because people did not think of him any more. They were not sure whether he existed, they just didn't think he needed to exist because they had no need of him. There were only a few people in The Trip who exhibited views as certain as those held by Hickling Laing. Most people did not want to appear extreme.

Drury was generally saddened by hearing these conversations. He almost preferred Hickling Laing's incalculable hatred of the idea of God, and his dedication to its total removal from Nottingham, to the limp statements of people who announced proudly their agnosticism. Drury knew that Hickling Laing faced a harder battle with apathy than he did with God or the violent words of Christians. Again, he found these things difficult to draw to Hickling Laing's attention. The most important part of his appearances to Hickling Laing, indeed the reason he had first done so, was to keep his friend happy. He admired the devotion to a cause that Hickling Laing brought to bear on his own life. But he was also amazed that someone with no belief in a friendly higher being could smile and possess such purpose. Drury could not actively help Hickling Laing in his battle to rid the city of God because he was not capable of agreeing that it should be done. But he decided not to obstruct Hickling Laing in his life's work. After all, he was only human.

Drury was sad at the decline of God but he was no supporter of the church.

He could not recall a time when he had not existed, though he'd not before had the name of Drury, and for as long as his memory he had seen God misrepresented by men and women. Always ulterior motives, threats, selfishness. These were the things that hurt him. He saw God trapped into stories, bound by the reasoning of people who could not even picture him, people who called on God as a last resort. The moans of centuries of human beings. And with increasing frequency, insults from atheists. He knew that God was powerless to avert disaster. He saw that God did not inflict sorrow and weeping on the distressed, and equally did not provide comfort. God was just an ordinary imaginary being, as wary of wise demons as anyone else. God had for eternity had his own life. It was a life of wandering. He was not responsible, not to blame, not to worship. He had no magic, no miracles. He had not created the world but had simply begun to live in it when it came to pass through random fusions of chemistry. Drury knew that God was an idea, a story, a shelter for weaknesses, a chamber in which to rejoice and remember. An invention and a truth.

When Drury had seen Hickling Laing drag the loud old man from the grip of God, he knew what was going on. It was true that Hickling Laing possessed a remarkable power in his eyes, that he could indeed free others from God. But Hickling Laing could not know what Drury knew. Through those black eyes he did not see that it was not God gripping the arm of the old man, but the man's own weaknesses. That is why he smiled, that is why he got up and walked. Hickling Laing had the depth of disbelief needed to give others the same, but he fought only the psychological dysfunctions of people. God did not enter battle.

It was a few months after Hickling Laing had started using the Angel Row library that Drury heard his voice and returned to him. Hickling Laing told him of all he had read: 95 novels, 151 short stories and 51 poems. The red chair had held him while he read and slept. It had become a place of experience and learning, the high wooden arms raising his own arms to a good reading position, the leather seat and back slipping him in and out of books. Hickling Laing said he had only read British literature; his task was great enough without taking on the rest of the world. He talked like this for hours, detailing plots, summarising epochs, listing characters and singing of fantasy and prophecy. All these had provided him with insights into why people love and hate, believe and disbelieve. And as Drury listened, Hickling Laing announced that he had come to a conclusion. He had decided that Nottingham did not need him, that the city was managing to avoid the grip of God on its own. He also thought it would be profitable to move to a bigger city. Drury already knew where this would be. Hickling Laing was going to take him to Birmingham.

This took a while to arrange. They had to find somewhere to live in Birmingham and dispose of the flat in Nottingham. However, on one of his very infrequent visits home, Hickling Laing's mother said that she would keep paying rent on the Nottingham flat for a month, just in case the move didn't work out and he wanted to come back to Nottingham. Hickling Laing, with his by now ferocious atheistic evangelism, thought this cautious and unnecessary but agreed. Secretly he was pleased though, because it meant he did not have to bring all his belongings. Early one morning Hickling Laing and Drury got on a train which pulled them under the castle, past the university and out of Nottingham towards the West Midlands.

Car had made this journey before them.

They watched as the Midlands flickered by the train window. Hickling Laing wondered why England, in the eyes of most people, was divided into halves. The North and The South. In this division lay the tension, competition and pride. But here he was forgotten, speeding between the two great Midlands cities, Birmingham its king and Nottingham its queen. The Midlands. A place of fantasy and construction. Of forms and revelry.

Hickling Laing and Drury could tell they had tracked within the boundaries of Birmingham. For miles on both sides of the train lay tower blocks, squat against the horizon of the city. As they closed into the centre, the massive barchart of central buildings looked to them at that moment more life-giving than the sky surrounding it. Birmingham is the only British city with an American skyline. Then they felt the train dip and slide under the buildings into darkness. Over the tannoy a syrupy accent said, *"Birmingham New Street. This is Birmingham New Street. All change for London, Edinburgh, Plymouth, Cardiff, Glasgow, Liverpool, Manchester, Leicester, Aberdeen, Bristol. Birmingham New Street. All change for internal Birmingham stations. Welcome to Birmingham New Street."*

They got out on platform 12 into a whirl, a juncture. The platforms curved underground and Hickling Laing stood staring through the gaps in the walls at this seemingly endless place of trains. They were tugged along by a rush for the escalators and onto them and up them. Drury jumped off the top into heaven. He really did think for a moment he was there. The same escalators, the same vast white room. He realised this was New Street Station though, because there were more people than were presently in heaven. Here was the hub that moved people around Britain, redirecting them, navigating them. But Hickling Laing and Drury were in the minority; they were staying. They went past the long row of security gates into another, this time higher, white space. New Street Station has the size and appearance of a major international airport.

They stepped onto more escalators and ascended again into The Palisades Shopping Centre, being carried between the shoulders of shoppers into the sun. When they came out there it was, the battleground, the marketplace of faith, the front line. New Street.

Hickling Laing and Drury glared up at the endless elegant facades. The shops glittered with costumes called fashion. Music played from every door and from street saxophonists or singers. Bedraggled painters knelt on the ground drawing large full colour reproductions in chalk of the faces of the famous: Elvis on one corner, Marilyn on another. Rain would run these icons into drains, only to be done again the next day. Food was being consumed on the black seats running the length of the street. It had come from countries all over the world, or at least been imitated from them. Everywhere, at ten metre intervals, someone sold God. He had been chopped into descriptions, opinions, angles. He was entangled in the weaknesses of all corners of the world. He suffered invocation by different names, and those involved in calling him vied with one another to see who could bring down his fire the sooner.

God walked unknown among them, saddened, for they knew not what they did.

Hickling Laing and Drury walked further up New Street towards Victoria Square, rounding into it. The City Hall stood over the square, magnificent in its width and light brown stone. Before it were a flight of steps ailed by water. The water ran its own steps down from a reclining abstract statue, a nude woman bathing in a huge pool. The 'floozie in the jacuzzi', as she was known in Birmingham. The two visitors to these shores continued past her and into Chamberlain Square. They fell under the shadow of Birmingham Central Library, rising like an upturned pyramid over a white statue of Chamberlain standing in his own pool. On the steep steps from the statue to the library an audience sat. On a plastic crate in front of them a Muslim sold the wares of Islam, bearded with no women in sight. He wore an ankle-length brown gown, and over it a padded jacket of orange and green proclaiming the dominance of some American football team. In this outfit he announced that all those passing him in beautiful suits were lost. Hickling Laing heard and moved on. He and Drury went into the belly of the library and looked up at two hundred feet of books. They stood, letting the world pass through the knowledge of the world.

Hickling Laing felt himself to be in the monstrance of the city. He had never been commanded by a building as he was then. Drury pulled him through expansive revolving doors to look out on the great length of Centenary Square. First, on either side the restaurants that sloped gently in black windows and red frames, then the shining white mausoleum where the forgotten dead are remembered, then grass and modern art and a Persian carpet of bricks. At the end, a quarter of a mile from the beginning, the glass and metal of Symphony Hall attached in kind to a skyscraper hotel. They walked the length of this, flanked by majestic buildings, and into the Symphony Hall Complex. More glass. More late twentieth century geometry. Then out the other side and beside the canals, more than Venice. Along them restaurants, clubs, pubs, jazz. They saw two hundred thousand pound apartments, oceans held in giant tanks, arenas for gladiators to display and grimace. Hickling Laing and Drury passed all this to another square, which had for its heart a restaurant made entirely of glass. Leading down to it were fifty jets of water, shooting five feet in the air. They walked between the water and sat down, ordering tea which came in glass cups. Glass and water. Birmingham for ninety pence.

After this drink they decided to go out of central Birmingham into the suburbs, where Hickling Laing had found a flat. Back through the squares to New Street and down onto platform eight. The green internal Birmingham train took them up from the station and north east, under the straining snakes of Spaghetti Junction to Gravelly Hill Station. It was then a five minute walk to the lake in Erdington which their flat looked across. The building contained many flats exactly the same in shape. They had been built with thin materials, and it was possible to hear the roar of nearby Spaghetti through the walls. This did not bother Drury, who was tired of keeping up an appearance and disappeared for the night. But Hickling Laing could not sleep. There was much on his mind, and the sound of traffic kept the population of his new city firmly at the front of it.

The next day he decided to start as he meant to finish, and took another green train down into New Street Station. He picked a prominent spot on New Street and began to talk. It was about lunchtime and the city was full and hungry. For a while people walked past him as they did all the street preachers, but soon, collectively, they began at least to hear him, if not actually listen. He talked of many things, of arriving in Birmingham only the day before to be met by so many people proclaiming to know God. He was subtle yet vicious, struggling to be heard above the famous street but making it. He drank water from a plastic bottle and kept going. A very small crowd attached themselves to his words and for the first time he had an audience. His voice had a clear Nottingham accent and it talked of literature. His argument to some may have seemed a little too proportioned for the task he had engaged, for he did not attack the group of young Christians performing mime a few metres away. He used stories as they did. Hickling Laing threw their technique back at them, the technique of fulfilment. Every member of the crowd who listened he affected, because while the Christians stated their own happiness they looked austere and inflated, but Hickling Laing appeared exactly as he said. Happy. He did not use the inventions of two thousand year old Palestinians, he quoted British literature. He proved that stories could battle stories and win. Hickling Laing showed the power of the human mind at work and people listened to it, thereby listening to themselves. Books became the bonds of community spirit, and community spirit the death of religion.

The young Christians had no answers to someone who asked them no questions. Hickling Laing resisted voicing all the trite and boring arguments for the non existence of God. Instead he blinded these young strays with the love between humans. He held them by the inexorable progression of literature, by things more ancient than God when humans were true hunters without weakness. Hickling Laing said that The Fall was not from a relationship with God, but was one of the imagination. We believed in God because we were too lazy to invent something else. Too judgmental. Too scared. He made one or two people cry and filled their minds with wonder. But he had not yet met the truly mad.

Later in the afternoon, when he had been talking for hours, three older Christians came to him and asked him to stop. He refused and it became an argument. They had been listening to him and picked out a weakness. He had no science. All he had was stories. Even his black stare could not work on them, they were too tightly bound in their idea of God. The Christians told him about the human body, and how much more remarkable it was than human stories. He could not argue with this, and did not understand the language of medicine to fight them. He gave up but was determined to find help.

When he got back to the flat he rang Birmingham University and was transferred to the Medical Library. He was by now quite used to librarians, and considered their advice the most useful. They were experts after all in the management of information. At the library, he spoke to someone else from Nottingham, another who had decided to leave, whose name was Car. Hickling Laing came across to Car as similar to himself, and they agreed to meet in the library.

Hickling Laing needed details and the library was the obvious source. He was due to go into Car's office at twelve o'clock but arrived a few minutes early, so he thought he may as well have a look around himself. Since leaving God and the devastation of his home in Nottingham, Car had suffered a great deal of trauma and was beginning to forget things. He would eventually forget his name. Sitting in his office, he noticed Hickling Laing searching the shelves of his library like a shark, gliding, banking, turning effortlessly. His were the movements of hunger and purpose, and he could do nothing but help someone kindred. He brought him into his office. Hickling Laing's first questions were full of energy but without skill. He had no language prepared for the complexity of medicine. They began to work together.

Hickling Laing told Car of his life's work, of why he had come to Birmingham. Car had never met someone with an atheism as fierce as his father's Christianity had once been, and immediately became intrigued by Hickling Laing's words. He also loved his eyes. Car had settled into the shape of men, and was often cut by their sharp jaws. A week later they planned to meet in Car's favourite pub in Birmingham, 'The Tap & Tumbler', to get to know one another. Hickling Laing spent the week reading and therefore ignoring Drury, who did not mind because he was busy wandering around Birmingham as he had done Nottingham.

'The Tap & Tumbler' nestles in Gas Street Basin, only feet from the water. Gas Street is to narrow boats what New Street is to trains. It too alters the directions of Britons.

They met. They drank. They were drunk. Hickling Laing told Car about Drury. He appeared and also became drunk. Car could not stop himself from telling Drury that he found him attractive. Drury knew already that Car would be the end of his loneliness. Love comes quickly to the desperate and the imaginary.

All three went back to the Erdington flat and drank dark red wine from cheap glasses. As a joke, Car stood with the wine and thanked God for his son who shed his blood on the cross so they might live. Drury laughed, but in a drunken piece of melodrama worthy of any evangelist, Hickling Laing stormed out. As soon as the door slammed, Drury and Car kissed deep into one another's mouths, falling in love.

Hickling Laing awoke the next morning happy but ashamed of his anger. He walked straight into Drury's room to apologise and found him asleep in the arms of Car. He left them and went out to preach. Despite a severe headache, he was happy that Car was giving Drury what he had never fully received himself, love and attention. On New Street his black eyes shone in the joy of disbelief.

My name is Tigguacobaucc. You may be as tired of that name as I am, but The Rings are still strong within me. They have a power even I did not realise was possible. I am misted but these stories are producing movement. I remember so much now, but not tendons or ligaments. The bones of my life are swinging freely and independent. I must try to build them into one story, my story. I remember a walk along the Trent with Black Boy, me breathing hard into my gloves, him following me. We crossed the suspension bridge and made it sway by jumping on the wooded slats. There were swans clumped under us on the water, quietly bobbing and on their marks to run from winter. From the suspension bridge it was only a short walk to the house, and we slung ourselves into its warmth. Before sleep, Black Boy told me that the River Trent derives its name from the Celtic word *Tristanton*, meaning trespasser, due to a long history of bank-breaking. I have felt that myself in my life, a trespasser. I remember thinking that I was in the wrong place, and it was wrong because it was not home. And stories can only be true when they are of home, when they are autobiography.

A person with no story is a diseased person. As is a person with too many.

For a few more days life continued this way. Hickling Laing had become well known on New Street. Car had brought books in the language of medicine for him to read and he had read them all. There was no-one who could read books faster. He had met the old Christians and won a memorable battle with them concerning the human body. They said it was a thing of miracles and must have been created. Hickling Laing showed the chemistry and physics that were its building blocks and held the Christians tight in his eyes. Two of them ran away thinking that his blackness and his sudden knowledge meant he must be Satan, but one of them did not. She could not run and underwent the great tugging between Hickling Laing and her idea of God. Eventually the Birmingham crowd witnessed Hickling Laing convert another Christian.

Car had decided to move into the Erdington flat as he lay awake beside the sleeping Drury. He had loved many people but never one of such softness. Drury had short black curly hair and strong facial features, which included large eyebrows. His body was very thin but perfect. Thick hair was on his legs, which ran like black water down his legs to carved ankles. He was not tall. His lips always parted. His eyes were brown and open like lakes. And Car saw that this was good.

There was no tension in the flat, even though Drury had come first to be a friend of Hickling Laing. There was something that bound all three, and it was home. They sat up one night late in the month and talked of Nottingham. Car had begun the discussion because he had seen a job in a library of medicine in Nottingham, and had applied. Drury told them he had loved wandering around a city that was so much bigger than Nottingham, but did not find Birmingham to be as responsive. This was a city built for the car. It was crossed by roads and junctions of a size impossible to construct in Nottingham. He could not hear himself think. Nor could he hear the thoughts of others. Hickling Laing said his heart had begun to distend every time he thought of Nottingham. He knew there was much work for him in Birmingham but he did not want to do it. He may be an evangelist but he was not mad, and would not destroy himself in arguments with others. Hickling Laing remembered that his mother had continued to pay rent for his flat on Mapperley Top. If they moved quickly, they might be able to keep it. He went out to find a phone, and while he was gone Car and Drury smoothed the angles of each other's bodies with their tongues. They jumped when the door closed after Hickling Laing and he came in and sat down. Drury held his breath because even he could not tell whether Hickling Laing was happy or otherwise. Hickling Laing said he had phoned his mother, told her their plans and asked her if the flat he loved, with the window over Nottingham, was still his. She had drawn her own breath and told him it was, and that he could come home.

This was good. But Car's sadness grew with his happiness.

Car's approach to loss had been to reach new heights of gregarity. He had opened his mind and ushered everyone who he could reach inside, where they were welcomed as saviours. Drury had become his real saviour, but he had lost as much as he had gained. Like Corner Pin, he'd received a letter from his father, telling him the details of distress. The father could not have known the effect of these letters. Corner Pin's sent him diving underground and Car, when he had finished reading it, developed confusion. Though his father's words brought him closer to his childhood, pushed memories in front of his face, they did not clear. Car was told things by his now millionaire mother that contradicted his father's words, and because he had been hidden from it all until it hit him, he had no way of knowing who was telling the truth.

His natural instinct was to believe his mother; after all, she was the injured party. It was his father who had done the leaving. But by this time his atheism had become more important to him than his parents. Car had discovered his own truth. And his mother, though less obviously involved with her own idea of God, still held one close to her breast. His father had dispensed with God entirely. His father said that he'd left the home in Nottingham as much to escape from the church as to love the woman with strong smelling skin. Car could feel nothing but approval for these words, and unlike in Corner Pin's letter, Car's father did talk to him about God. He made the mistake of thinking only Car was old enough for philosophy. The father said that instead of harvesting and thanking God for his goodness, he had learned to fill his new south coast garden with flowers. They were of no use. They could not be eaten. They appeared only for a short time. They required a higher level of patience. He grew them only for the sake of their beauty, and so he had stumbled upon the reason for the existence of the earth—that there was no reason for its existence.

Car knew all of this and knew it to be true.

As he thought back over his childhood he could no longer distinguish between invention and truth. Because the details were becoming increasingly blurred, so was the big picture. And the big picture in Car's eyes was his name. Was that an invention or a truth? He no longer knew. The most tangible thing he had left was his love for an imaginary being. This would confuse anyone.

Hickling Laing dozed under New Street. The train pulled from the dark sub-city station into the suburbs of Birmingham and out of them. He felt he had not wasted time. He remembered the days when he was younger and living in a lonely world, but happy there. Hickling Laing remembered his first favourite place, Woodthorpe Drive, sweeping down from Mapperley Top into Sherwood. He saw himself standing at the Mapperley end, thinking about his city, looking at the view across all of north-west Nottingham. He had looked over his home town and seen it through his black eyes. But he had not been loved at home. When he was young and standing like this with Nottingham as far as the eye could see, he'd made the mistake of believing that because he was not loved then he could not love, and if he was unable to love somewhere then he could not lose it. This logic had taken him away from Nottingham and was now returning him. He had wondered if Nottingham really was the place in which he could be happiest. Hickling Laing discovered he was not diseased. He had only one story. One place.

It would be a squash, but Car, who returned to Nottingham without a name and with mist in his eyes, had decided to move in with Hickling Laing and Drury on Mapperley Top. They were all happy with this arrangement.

The train pulled in, and Hickling Laing woke Drury and Car who slept opposite him. They looked sleepily around and then out of the window. There was the sign. NOTTINGHAM.

Here was home. Here was the place which dreams are made on. Under the famous castle the city rolled in its legends, displayed its outlaws, became more beautiful, hid another city beneath it. The three men—one evangelist, one librarian, one imaginary being—climbed the steps and walked from the station to the centre. They moved down Carrington Street and over the canal, waiting for the blur of traffic to stop so they could cross Collin Street. They walked beside the Broadmarsh Shopping Centre and through a right-angled underpass into the shopping centre itself. There were hundreds of people in the cafe in the square, talking of busy lives or coveting those of others. Drury heard it all. They came out onto Lister Gate, and as they pushed their way up it, the dome of The Council House came into view above the roofs of shops and offices. They went past St Peter's Church, quiet after eight hundred years, and crushed them-selves into the crush of Exchange Walk, the busiest path in Europe.

They reached the top of the Walk and came out on South Parade, facing, under the columns of The Council House, Old Market Square. It had been less than a month since they had left Nottingham, but they looked on the expansive heart of the city as if it literally pumped the nutrients in their blood. From the air, Old Market Square is a vast lake of pavement with four islands. Two of these are covered in grass, and two are fountains. The lake is banked by South Parade and Long Row. In spring and summer, flowers sit all over the square like waterlilies, hanging only for their beauty. The Council House rides the lake like a great white ship, balanced by lions.

Hickling Laing led the prodigals across the lake to a bus, which took them from this heart up the vein of Woodborough Road to Mapperley Top. Hickling Laing's mother was waiting outside the flat with his key. There was no malice in her. She smiled at him, gave him the key and left. Car had never seen anything like it; his own mother would have caressed him violently. Car had been away from Nottingham much longer, long enough to become a professional librarian. He had decided just to let things between his parents run their own course; he was going to try from now on to stay healthy. This meant putting his efforts into his own life and not worrying about or comparing the lives of his mother and father. He had come to this conclusion because he believed this to be his parent's attitude towards Corner Pin and himself.

Corner Pin. Car did not know what had happened to him. Though there had been more than distance between them over the past few years, Car still desperately wanted to see his brother.

The three friends organised the flat around this new number. Hickling Laing kept the back room and the other two slept together at the front. Drury began again to walk around Nottingham, more determined than ever to see its entire architecture. Car started a new job in a medical library on the other side of the city. Hickling Laing spent the first week sitting in his flat feeling home move around him like heat. He and Drury had not had much time together without Car, so Hickling Laing took the chance to ask Drury about him.

Hickling Laing: *Does Car love you, Drury?*
Drury: *Yes. He tells me so.*
Hickling Laing: *What is it about you that he loves?*
Drury: *My ability to be near him at all times. I am always close.*
Hickling Laing: *You're with him now aren't you, even though you're also with me?*

Drury: *Yes, you are both talking to me.*

pause

Hickling Laing: *Look at my eyes. They were born black.*
Drury: *I know, I've looked often.*
Hickling Laing: *You know also that I don't believe in God?*
Drury: *Yes.*
Hickling Laing: *And that I hate the idea of him?*
Drury: *Yes.*
Hickling Laing: *And that I love you?*
Drury: *Yes. And that I love you.*

They talked for the whole day. They watched the sun turn the north-west view pink and orange. Drury sat on the bed, and Hickling Laing sat on the red chair. It was quiet between them for a while, and then Drury told Hickling Laing all the great secrets that he knew, and his own great secret. He told Hickling Laing what he knew of God. He told him God was just an ordinary imaginary being, as wary of wise demons as anyone else. Drury told of the random fusions of chemistry, and of God's wandering life. He said God was powerless to avert disaster, and that he never brought disaster about. God had never sat in judgment. God was not what Christians understood him to be. Hickling Laing responded by believing every word Drury said.

Hickling Laing: *But why do Christians weep when they are caught in my eyes?*
Drury: *Because until then they have only been caught in themselves.*
Hickling Laing: *But what of the faith they profess?*
Drury: *It is a barrier between their own weakness and the world.*
Hickling Laing: *That is why people become Christians at the lowest point of their lives?*

Drury: *Yes. It is an escape route.*
Hickling Laing: *And one without foundation?*
Drury: *If they believe God is their foundation then yes, they build their faith on sand.*
Hickling Laing: *How can you be sure? Many things are unfounded.*
Drury: *Because I am only known as Drury in your story. I am in all stories.*
Hickling Laing: *So, are you an invention or a truth?*
Drury: *All real stories are both.*
Hickling Laing: *But you are imaginary. How can you understand the needs of humans?*
Drury: *I lost someone who claimed to be my son, many years ago. He was brave.*
Hickling Laing: *Is it the man who called himself Jesus Christ?*
Drury: *Yes. He was so brave even I believed him. He was made only of good thoughts.*

Hickling Laing could not believe what he saw, but he could believe what he was hearing. He had devoted his life so far to proclaiming aloud that God did not exist. He had been right to tell people this, because they worshipped something that did not want their worship. They believed God could perform acts he could not perform. They accepted the words of a man who had merely been brave, and had used his words to stand in judgment over others. They had listened to inventions and understood them to be truths. Hickling Laing had pointed his fingers at all of these errors and now he had proof. When he was a child he had called for a companion and his call had been answered like a prayer.

Hickling Laing: *When I was young and lonely, you came to me.*
Drury: *I came because I was lonely too.*
Hickling Laing: *But why me? You must hear millions of lonely voices.*

Drury: *I chose you because you didn't believe, you would never use me to harm others.*
Hickling Laing: *My black eyes. Did you give them to me?*
Drury: *I've told you, I cannot perform miracles. I can only know when they happen.*
Hickling Laing: *Like the birth of the man who said he was your son?*
Drury: *Yes. I knew that had happened without a father, but I did not cause it.*
Hickling Laing: *And are you still lonely?*
Drury: *No. I have you as a friend and Car as a lover.*

Car left work that evening keen to have the scent of another man near him. He knew the reputation of The Forest and took a bus up Mansfield Road instead of Woodborough Road, getting off beside a disused Greek-style house. He walked down the long avenue of pink stones under the austere orange lights and turned up into the area of trees, away from where Goose Fair sits in October. He moved with nonchalance. He caught the eyes of a nervous young man. He walked over to him and put his arms around him. They kissed. This was not love but it was still something. A runner, moving fast enough to overtake the wind, rushed past, glimpsing Car's face amongst the trees.

Car finished in The Forest and decided to walk back to Mapperley Top. He crossed the huge roundabout where in October a giant white goose sits, and walked up Mansfield Road to Sherwood. He climbed the steep inclines of Winchester Street and Mapperley Rise, surfacing on Woodborough Road. Then it was a short walk along Plains Road to Greengate Avenue and home.

When he opened the door he called out for Hickling Laing and Drury. There was no answer, so he went through to the back room. In there a small but important change had taken place. Hickling Laing was sitting on his bed, and Drury sat on the red chair.

Car: *What is happening?*
Hickling Laing: *Remember when you were a child and you loved God?*
Car: *Yes. But I put away those childish things and became a man.*
Hickling Laing: *I didn't believe it at first, but things are not what they seem.*
Car: *In Nottingham things never are.*
Hickling Laing: *No, but God has something to say to you.*
Drury: *Hello Car. I love you.*

The red chair squatted there in its red leather. It was old and cheap and low to the ground, but Drury seemed to like it. There was much to talk about and it held him well. A red chair was all it took to make him comfortable. Drury had no pecuniary needs, and being comfortable was all it took to make him talk. He had less to say than Hickling Laing and Car expected, but after all, Drury was only an ordinary imaginary being.

My name is Tigguacobaucc and I have heard all this and retold it in order to discover my real name, my own story. But God moves in mysterious ways, and I still have no beginning and no ending. My story is still a genuine mish-mash. And your back is still against the sandy walls of Tigguacobaucc, leaning under Nottingham. Waiting. Breathing in the air around the pillars ten metres down. Waiting. Hickling Laing and Drury are close to me because they too have come from a different city, Birmingham, and become stuck with loving this one. To be honest, at the end, my story could easily be told through theirs. I think I've let that happen.

An invention and a truth.

Car suggested that the three of them should go out. They all walked through Nottingham, down Mansfield Road towards the city itself. The city shimmered in history and modernity. There is immense life here, contained within a name, held above and below. Two parts. Drury said that he knew of a second part to Nottingham, an underground place of caves.

Car: *How do you know?*
Drury: *I once fled from it.*
Car: *Why?*
Drury: *Someone was calling a wise demon.*
Car: *And you were wary?*
Drury: *The demon believes me to be evil.*
Hickling Laing: *But you love Car. You love me.*
Drury: *The demon mistakes the words of Christians for my words.*

pause

Car: *How did you escape him?*
Drury: *I rode the call between the teeth of the caller.*
Car: *Whose teeth?*
Drury: *Your brother's.*

Drury took them to the Peel Street entrance. They went down the steps in the sandstone, and on into the vaulted labyrinth. They could hear Nottingham above them, living the night. Hickling Laing stroked the walls with his fingers, and some of the surface fell away into a small pile of sand by his feet. He thought how easy it must be to carve caves from this; it was barely stone at all. Drury heard him and told him it was simple to make a small pile near the feet, but hard to make a flight of steps, and harder still to make a labyrinth. These caves, he said, had taken two hundred years to appear. He had watched from the ever darkening shadows, as the man who did it pushed further under the city. The effort of carving his own maze meant that this man was always angry. He now has a withered face which no-one wishes to see.

It was quiet underground, but not silent. Noises happened. Drury could not tell whence they originated. He said that though sound travels fast, it is a living thing. Unlike him, sound could not pass through sandstone. It rebounded from the pillars and arches, and there were so many of these down here that the sound could resonate, propelled by its environment, for years. It could take as much time to reach their ears as light from a distant star will take above ground, in the other city. Hickling Laing and Car responded by believing only some of these words.

Tap. Tap. Tap. They walked on in the darkness, led only by the sound of someone working the sand. The tapping grew closer, and in the distance there was a yellow light. They walked quicker now, towards the light. It became a shadow on the wall around a massive pillar which splayed on the roof of the cave, holding it up. They stopped and peered. With his back to them, an ancient figure sat beside a candle, removing sand from beneath Nottingham. He heard Drury whispering to Hickling Laing and Car, and turned to face them. They looked at his face and turned away. Behind them, a lean young man stood, out of breath. Hickling Laing and Drury took a few steps back, but Car and Corner Pin moved so close as to almost touch, immediate but strangers.

chapter 5

the story of rouse

*N*OTTINGHAM. *August 1801. James Rouse digs the ground for the first time. He digs out a step six inches lower than Peel Street, and then another. Six inches lower again. Another. Rouse opens a wound in the skin of the city which incurs the lash to his endless life; a pillared maze dug ten metres down, worked from ten thousand tons of sand. He is still digging.*

In the nineteenth century Rouse has a smooth face and is not unusual. Many men stand in rags and dig the surface of Nottingham. It is not a race, for that would be madness, but they keep their eyes on each other. New sand is a rich commodity, and Nottingham is a sea bed being struck for oil.

Rouse does not work incessantly, because he loves a jocose girl called Ann. Each evening he stops digging and calls her to drink with him. They get drunk in The Trip to Jerusalem, which is bored into the rock of the Castle. Ann sings sweet as a jay in Sherwood Forest.

The young lovebirds sit in a seat that ballads have it once caressed the legendary arse of Robin Hood himself, and the commonest song Ann sings is a jeremiad on the death of the famous outlaw. On the wall behind her pretty head is an arrow shot in the song and hung in The Trip by Little John as a present to the publican. Ann opens her mouth and quietness falls.

> *"But give me my bent bow in my hand,*
> *And a broad flo I'll let flee,*
> *And where the same shall be taken up*
> *My grave shall digged be.*
>
> *Lay me this bright sword at my head,*
> *These arrows at my feet;*
> *And lay this yew-bow by my side*
> *That made me music sweet.*
>
> *Let me have length and breadth enough,*
> *With a green sod under my head,*
> *That they may say, that pass my grave:*
> *'Here Robin Hood lieth dead!'*
>
> *He's done him to the shot-window,*
> *And wondrous far he shot;*
> *Though the flo it sped four hundred yards,*
> *Little John he missed it not.*
>
> *Then Robin he yielded up the ghost,*
> *That no word more spake he.*
> *But Little John his grave hath digged—*
> *It was hard by Kirkeslie."*

Though the patrons hear Ann every night, their ale is always downed in one for the famous son of Nottingham. Rouse gets Ann from the tabletop and sits her on his knee. He can feel her heat rising and it warms him. They leave the pub and walk through the town, kissing on every corner. Rouse tells Ann he cannot believe in Robin Hood, even though she sings of him with passion in her heart. Ann smiles because she has told him a thousand times that the story of Robin is true. Ann thinks all real stories are a stew of invention and truth. One will not exist without the other. She is kissed goodnight on the steps Rouse is digging to a labyrinth, already a place for bodies to slide against other bodies. They kiss another six inches below Nottingham each night, but the stars in their sidereal hair mark them by the speed of light.

The face of the Sheriff of Nottingham changes fifty times and Ann lies dead.

Rouse holds her withered body in his withered arms. He sits her on his knee and opens her mouth. There is no life exiting. He drops her to the ground and the force pushes the last words in her brain out on the last air in her lungs: 'But Little John his grave hath digged.' Rouse takes a bow and shoots an arrow out of sight. He lifts his wife of fifty years and searches for the arrow. When he finds it, he lays Ann down and digs a grave for her. At least, he thinks, she can hear Goose Fair from here.

Nottingham. October 1901. Rouse walks up from The Forest and onto Peel Street. His cave has provided for Ann in many ways and now he will join her underground. He picks up his tools but cannot call her to drink with him, so descends the many steps into the vaults he has dug and continues digging. He hacks hard at the rock but without passion, for there is no-one to respond to it, no singing in the shadows on the sand. His face withers over decades and the skin collapses his eyes.

Nottingham. August 2001. A man sits at the sand-face of a labyrinth. His digging throws angry shapes in the candlelight. People use the place he is digging but cannot look upon his withered features. He has become angry. They do not know why. They will be glad to be rid of him. He does not know why. But among shadows a famous ghost talks to Rouse about archery and two arrows hang in The Trip.

chapter

the story of old angel

OLD Angel is not afraid of the sky falling on his head, but he is wary of the city above him. His ears are perked towards the roofs of caves and his eyes watch for slight shudders. He believes vibrations will be the death of him. He is convinced the caves, Tigguacobaucc, will one day be filled with concrete, covering us cowering within them. My name is Tigguacobaucc and I do not think this will happen. Old Angel, I'll reveal now, is the most important part of my life.

Old Angel, who is neither, is a reader of books, and though he does not write them, it was his idea that I should tell our stories. He is worried about concrete filling our hiding places, but does he mean actual concrete or is he using concrete as an exaggeration of stale air. The purpose of these stories is to clear the air around me—to enable my recall. Old Angel is well known for his use of metaphor. Can he be trusted? Can I be trusted? Can we trust each other? Ah, The Rings. Either way, whichever way, under or over way, exaggeration comes in many forms and in all of them it is an underrated virtue. So in the end, at his very worst, Old Angel is merely a virtuous liar.

Old Angel is a son of Nottingham but, like most of us, does not yet have his own ballad. Could these stories one day be seen as ballads for their owners? I will not live long enough to know.

Youth is the largest group here. Old Angel is a man in his early fifties, and in an environment dug by the still digging Rouse that is young. Sometimes he wears a moustache, which suits him; but often he does not wear it, which suits him. He carries a little too much weight. He is not tall. Old Angel began without significant dreams but was a dreamer nonetheless.

When I first met him in Nottingham I felt sure I had met him before, but such was the strength of my Rings I could not remember. Whether I had known him or not, Old Angel treats me like his own son. He is not the most attentive father I have felt walking beside me. I cannot remember my real father at all, but I picture him being weaker than my mother. Old Angel spotted me in the caves when I arrived in Nottingham without a name. We talked for an entire night and he became the most important person in my life for two reasons: he seemed to know more about me than I did myself; he gave me the name of the place that held us, Tigguacobaucc. One more thing—these words are his words:

A person with no story is a diseased person. As is a person with too many.

As I have told you already what I can remember of my own story, I will tell you what Old Angel has told me of his.

Old Angel has never been rich. His family lived in an unusual area in Nottingham. It could be called second-rate and is known as Sneinton. The family could also be called second-rate if they had lived in a house. Old Angel was born in a cave. This was not usual but possible.

There are three kinds of cave in Nottingham. Sand mines like the one Rouse continues are huge but infrequent. Most buildings in the city centre, especially pubs, have caves beneath them as storerooms. Finally there are cave houses, distinct from stores because they are entered horizontally into steep slopes or cliffs of the sandstone. Traveller's tales from 1610 and 1639 tell stories of most of the people of Nottingham living underground. It has been said that these stories are inventions, but I have told you what stories must be made on. In Lenton, just west of the castle, there are dwellings in the low cliff on the southern edge of The Park estate. These caves are known as Lenton Hermitage and once included the chapel of St Mary de la Roche. They were the property of Lenton Priory, founded around 1100. It is written that two monks lived in these caves in 1244. It is not written that they were in love. Most of history goes unrecorded, and I only know this because they were once visited by Drury. In 1651 the hermitage was sacked by Roundhead soldiers, but five caves survived the violence, each opening at the foot of the cliff. In 1962 one of these was being used as an office, but they are all hidden now by the garages of Castle Boulevard. It is assumed that after all this history Lenton Hermitage is lost and wounded, but there are more rumours about the disuse of Tigguacobaucc than there are of its use. In the cave where two monks once held one another against the darkness, Jalland crawls from one influence only to buckle beneath another.

Another influence, another hermitage. Old Angel entered the strange world of these two cities not in Lenton but in Sneinton Hermitage. Like its cousin west of the castle, the hermitage at Sneinton is carved into cliffs. Many of the caves were destroyed in three phases of railway construction and road widening. Very few remain but records tell of these rock houses as early as 1518. It is thought that people stopped living in them about a hundred years ago. This is a few metres from the truth. For three hundred metres the cliff face follows the road. The relationship used to be reversed but the cliff has been pulled down to widen the road. Many houses fell with the cliff but some held, holding their families cowering within them. The last time the road was widened, Old Angel and his family huddled in the back room determined to survive or die with their house. It was all they had. Old Angel can remember the sound of falling rock. He can recall the actions of surface people who did not care what they did to the city beneath their own. It is reasonable that he believes vibrations will be the death of him. They were once the death of his own father.

The house was small. It contained three rooms, none more than three metres across. The first room ran about ten metres back from the cliff face, doubling as a sitting room and kitchen. Leading from a hole halfway along the wall was a bedroom for Old Angel's parents. His mother's name was Joyce and his father's Burton. Another hole cut near the back of the main room was a bedroom for Old Angel and his sister, Ena. This family had not built the cave, for it was much older than they were, but they added to it as necessary. Burton cut shelves and niches into the walls, and where possible cut carefully sited openings to let light into the recesses. Though this was a cave, it had some ordinary fittings. There was a chimney to flow smoke from the cliff face, doors and even windows in some of the cuttings. In Sneinton railways were more violent than the Roundheads and the need for tracks through the east of the city was deemed more important than houses in the rock. Many caves were lost to the erosion of trains.

But between the railway cutting of 1896 at the western end of the cliff face and the railway cutting of 1903 at the eastern end, some caves did survive. This is where Old Angel experienced family life. Burton worked behind the bar at The Earl Manvers pub. A loud and aggressive job, but one he enjoyed. Like Old Angel he was a stocky man and pulling pints was not a problem to his thick arms. The people who used The Earl Manvers were raw. Sneinton could be seen as deepest Nottingham, far from the heights of elegance, of carriages drawn by eight horses through the great tunnel from Derby Road to The Park. Here lived the people who worked the city, whose parents and grandparents had over centuries carved Tigguacobaucc for their own use or for the use of the rich. They spoke with firm Nottingham accents. One famous story concerning a Saturday night and Sunday morning of some of these people has made them well known, but there is more to Nottingham than work. This city contains things more magical than ordinary lives, though the magical is ordinary here.

Magic is the art of inventing the truth.

Old Angel's mother worked behind the bar in another pub, The White Swan. Joyce did not have the thick arms of her husband, but her skin was the equal of his and she too enjoyed her job. Joyce was taller than Burton. Joyce loved Old Angel more than Ena. Joyce did not make a secret of this. She treated her son delicately though he was not delicate. She served Old Angel as she did the patrons of The White Swan. He was a spoilt brat with no money.

Ena on the other hand was required to act in a way Joyce thought all women should act. From an early age she washed clothes, cooked meals and swept the sand that constantly fell from the walls. All of this was for the benefit of Old Angel. Burton wouldn't have noticed either way. When she was young Ena did these things with a light heart. When she was older she held all men responsible for the lack of fun in her youth.

Old Angel never knew any different from this life. He grew up expecting women to serve him, to keep hats on their heads and their mouths shut.

He was not exceptional, but from childhood had a talent up his sleeve. In public Old Angel was always a great speaker. A small man with a big voice. Due to the security of volume in his voice people thought Old Angel more intelligent than he really was. Joyce led this opinion. She had no ambitions for Ena because Ena was a girl, but for Old Angel her ambition was limitless. It was also without perspective because anything he did was regarded by his mother as genius. Things could not have been different if he'd been an only child, except that he could not have hurt a brother or sister. As they were, Ena watched from the corner of the cave they called home and chronicled the effect of wearing a pair of trousers.

As a child, if anyone was to blame for his behaviour it must be Joyce. As an adult he had to learn to take responsibility for his own actions, but as he had never been taught this he made many mistakes before becoming the wise creature I know him to be. Old Angel is neither and nor is he a demon, so unlike demons he was not born with wisdom.

Sneinton Hermitage served him as well as the women of his house. His father's friends referred to him as the youngest hermit in Nottingham, for Old Angel was never without books. He was skilled in a library at the age of ten and by his mid teens he had read more stories than anyone in Sneinton. Though these people were poor this was a greater achievement than it first seems. The inhabitants of Sneinton Hermitage were all like me. They made their life within pungence. This is what caves and libraries have in common: they are often corners. I love them both and so did Old Angel and his neighbours. It was not competitive, but in these houses in the cliff, stories were consumed like cream cakes.

Old Angel has always cultivated a habit of sulking. He is more relaxed now than he has ever been, but for much of his life he sought attention from others by ignoring them. At home this was effective management of his mother's feelings because she considered his silences as manifestations of a great brain. As I said, he was a spoilt brat. This was a problem for everyone who met him as a man, because as a child he had been treated like one. Until late in life his periods of immaturity and maturity came in the wrong order. When he possessed his own muscles and hair he acted as though they were not yet there.

This immature nature, combined with his extortionate use of women, turned him into a perfect man: flawed but flaunting. He performed his first marriage like an exequy.

The life in a cosy cave looked unshakeable, as all simple things look. But complexity waits like a lion in the grass, waiting to pounce and rip. Behind the bar of The Earl Manvers, Burton was quick and smooth. After hours in front of it he took to emptying pints into himself, rather than the stomachs of others. It began with one for the very short road back to the Hermitage. It ended by pressure on the heart that no heart can withstand. And the end came when Old Angel was eleven and Ena nine.

Ena and Burton would have thought alike, if only she'd been allowed to think like a man. But in the true English tradition she made do with what she had, and that was a father who came home drunk and late every night. Joyce did nothing to stop this because she believed her husband, as a working man, should be able to relax when work finished. It didn't occur to her that she did the same job and never relaxed. Ena would lie awake in the same room as her brother, waiting for the heavy sounds of her father. The steps. The breathing. She would run and sit down on him when he sat down and he would tell her stories. Off his tongue, on high alcohol breath he told Ena of princes and princesses, of the miles of tunnels stretching under Nottingham, of Robin Hood and Maid Marian and the secret woes of Merry Men. He made her jump, he made the tiny hairs on her arms stand like needles on her skin. He made her eyes bright then tearful, her legs wobble then the next moment, primed for adventure. He dropped from a shout to a whisper in a second. In his armchair, Burton was on stage. Up there he was brilliant and exciting and safe.

On stage he was a real father.

In his bed in the next room, Old Angel listened to every inflection and learnt the tricks of what would for a while become his trade. He heard Ena returning to her bed and was not jealous of what she had with Burton because he knew what he had with Joyce. Isaiah Ch.12 V.9 came into his head: *'They shall not hurt nor destroy in all my holy mountain: for the earth shall be full of the knowledge of the Lord, as the waters cover the sea.'* At age eleven Old Angel lay his head peacefully because he had begun to read the Bible.

In Sneinton Hermitage libraries were pillaged for stories. They were not used for any other reason. Access to information has improved in the years of Burton and Joyce, but when Burton needed information he would not have been able to use my medical library. The university staff would have looked at his tell-tale red face, his sandy clothes and known he was an alcoholic from Tigguacobaucc. But he would not even have known about a library of medicine, because doctors back then believed even less in empowering patients with knowledge than they do now. When Burton visited his doctor, he was simply told to cut down on the drink and take some exercise. He complained of chest pains but the doctor, seeing from the pile of sand on the floor that Burton lived in a cave, just thought he deserved it.

Because they both pulled pints in old-fashioned pubs, Burton and Joyce were home for much of the day and they received no warning. They were lying in bed when vibrations took hold of Burton's heart. As I retell what Old Angel has told me, I remember Black Boy's questions on the language of medicine. All he knew was that he was building a heart and he needed a blueprint. I did not possess his manual dexterity but I could speak the language, so we began to work together. I first provided him with information on coronary anatomy, and encouraged him to think of the heart in angiographic views, to think in great detail. This took time, but he gradually recognised the right and left coronary systems at both right and left anterior oblique views. The branches of the two principal coronary arteries: sinoatrial, lateral, obtuse marginal, medial circumflex, circumflex, atrioventricular and septum expanded in Black Boy's brain until he could begin to construct a heart in his living room.

The building of Black Boy's heart continued, until after a time it existed enough for me to warn of the diseases that could strike it. I carried books over Trent Bridge that told of the frailty of hearts. One book described angina pectoris, a central crushing chest pain which may radiate to the jaw, neck or one or both arms. It is precipitated by exertion, anxiety, cold weather and heavy meals. It is relieved by rest and nitrates.

Another book contained words on myocardial infarction, the death of heart muscle. The pain in this case is usually of greater severity and duration than in angina, and associated with great distress. To watch here are the painless infarcts which can kill in silence. It is strange how the definitions of medical words can sound as though they are defining the emotional as well as the spiritual.

Endocardium. The inner lining of the heart.

In bed, Burton lay on his back and Joyce lay on her side with her back to him. She felt the shudders of the cliff face shake the walls of their home. She did not see Burton clutch his chest, or his eyes spring open. She couldn't possibly have seen the inner lining of his heart infarct beyond repair. Joyce did see that her husband was dead. She rushed outside and looked down to the street beneath the cliff. Men were widening the road, hacking at the rock face. She screamed at them over the noise of their machines. They shouted back that it would be alright, they would do no damage to her home.

Ena and Old Angel were told their father was dead when they came back from school. Joyce sat them in the main room of the cave. She had called an elder to come from the local church. All three sat in the sandy room and heard Joyce recount. Old Angel watched his mother cry, and cried himself. His father had never held him and whispered special things in his ear, but he knew also that any chance of that ever happening was now gone. But Ena felt Burton's absence pull at the inner lining of her heart immediately. Burton had been to her what he had never been to Old Angel. This was a Monday, and only the night before, Burton had sat in his armchair proclaiming stories.

The teenage years of Ena and Old Angel were very similar to those of their childhood, if perhaps more exaggerated. Life became easier for Old Angel at home because not only was he turning into a man, he was the only one. It was his head at the forefront of the cave. He did little to deserve this. He brought in no money because Joyce thought his time would best be spent reading books. Old Angel was without reck for Ena. She, in fact, was cleverer than he was, but pointing a finger with a duster in your hand did not look clever so she never did it. There were many chores associated with living in a five hundred year old house, and Old Angel did not lift a finger.

His father's dissension from life affected his own belief in God. It became stronger and more private. He could not face the familiar faces at what had once been the family church because, just as they had always asked him how school was going, they now asked him if he was alright, if he was coping. He did not have an answer to these questions. Old Angel was amazed at the dry canyon left by someone who had hardly been there for him in the first place. What surprised him and his mother was that he did not turn to her for comfort. He retired even further from family life and searched himself. Though only young, he became deeply involved with himself, and grew sadder each day. Sadness he believed to be the correct tower from which to view himself, but he was always forced to climb higher as his view was constantly obscured by clouds.

The size of things is what youth is all about.

Old Angel was eighteen when he fell in love for the first time. The vicar of his church had brought his family up to Nottingham from the West Country. The vicar was unremarkable and his wife was the opposite. She was much taller than him and walked with the confidence of the talented. The vicar's name was Arthur and his remarkable wife was called Port. He was an average preacher. She had fingers that could transform any material into anything.

They had three daughters: one large, one formidable, one flowery. These daughters were all destined to marry vicars themselves, though one of them turned out happier than the others by losing her vicar and ascending the faces of cliffs. And the first cliff face to feel the weight of her feet was Sneinton Hermitage.

Old Angel had watched her across the church from the moment she arrived in Nottingham. She was the formidable daughter, but she was also small. Her hair was brown and tickled her shoulders. Her eyes were brown, a common thing, and her mouth was wide, an uncommon thing. She was very pretty. Old Angel saw in her both a challenge and a lack of challenge. It would not be hard to control her body because she was even smaller than him, but it would be difficult to control a tongue that spoke from such a large cavern. But these were not the first things he saw. At the beginning it was love and Old Angel's love was called Victoria.

The first time Victoria visited Sneinton Hermitage Joyce took her to one side and told her of Old Angel's habit. He would sit in his father's armchair and sulk. Victoria had determined a hidden temper within Old Angel, but the charm that veiled the temper covered her too. Joyce said that he could maintain a silence all evening if he wished, and as he was a young man without significant dreams this was usually all he wished for. Victoria listened to Joyce, but thought she knew one aspect of his character that his mother could not know about. When Old Angel took her out in Nottingham he never sulked. They would often cycle from Sneinton along Castle Boulevard and into Lenton, where there was a small cinema away from the crowds of the city. Old Angel delighted Victoria when they were young. It was a match made in Sneinton but tied in Birmingham.

Everyone said they would get married. Everyone was right. No one could hear the vows being said over the industrial steam and clatter.

Old Angel wore a grey suit. Victoria bought a very short mint-green dress and a wide hat to match. They were married by Arthur, Victoria's father. The sun was high and bright in the sky. Not much money was involved because there was not much money about. Old Angel has said that, looking back, everyone seemed young, even the grandparents; it seems now to be such a different, long-past world. He remembers the wind being strong that day. It buffeted them. But Old Angel and Victoria were grounded firmly in each other and they had a plan. They had decided where their marriage would take off, and were so happy in the decision that they went to their first house together for their honeymoon. The house sat in a famous leafy suburb of the famous industrial city, Edgbaston.

Victoria got a job as a teacher in a busy primary school. She often had more than forty kids in her class, young all of them. Old Angel began messing about with engineering of some kind, and though he was not possessed by significant dreams he was a dreamer nonetheless. Things began to go wrong very quickly. It can only be guessed why engineering lost its potential to fulfil Old Angel's small dreams. The tangibility of steel is probably to blame: it was too definite and cold. All his life, Old Angel had sat in a cave reading books and being waited on hand and foot by two women. And now here he was in a massive and strange city, bottom of a large pile of oily men and with a wife who was skilled and respected in her work. A wife without the time or inclination to pamper him. Whatever happened he was an engineering apprentice who decided to exchange the spanner for the pulpit and start to fiddle instead with the mysterious workings of God.

Corner Pin has shown me old photographs of Victoria and Old Angel together in Birmingham, for some reason enhanced by my own knowledge of the city. Wait. My name is Tigguacobaucc and I have a knowledge of Birmingham even though I cannot remember ever being there. Wait. I am moved by Corner Pin's old pictures. Certainly I know and love Old Angel now, but back then? I have no emotion for his past, only his present. My name is Tigguacobaucc and I am being moved by things I did not experience, by people I did not know. If I also did not know about The Rings I would swear I am remembering things. I would swear the air is clearing, slow and sure.

Whatever happened Old Angel chose God instead of metal, an idea over steel. He followed God until God had placed a collar around his neck. This collar, white against smooth grey suits, was all Old Angel needed to live. But this is not to say that it was honourable or simple. Old Angel cannot remember why he went into engineering in the first place, but it was probably because he needed to earn money. He had planned to complete his apprenticeship, and as well as providing for himself and Victoria, he would send money back to Sneinton for his mother. None of this happened, though he was in the right place at the right time. Birmingham still produced and constructed for the world. He was unskilled but could easily have become skilled. What his new honeymoon life lacked was the respect he had grown used to at home. In Birmingham he was a nobody. People did not fall over themselves to serve him and he would do anything to re-establish that status quo.

Here their flying began.

Old Angel called his attempt to get people to serve him again a 'call from God,' and by doing so he instantly gained credibility. From the day he set down his first book in the cave, Old Angel had a talent for wordplay. Another word for wordplay is lies. He told Victoria that though engineering is complex work it can be understood, and he did not want to involve himself in a subject with clearly defined points of entry and re-entry, specific drives for specific screws. He told Victoria that God had provided him with tools he could not hold and bits of belief that were impossible to piece together. He told her that she must support him as he trained to become a minister. She must bring in the money. And this was love.

And this was love because it was what he wanted—unending complexity— a world where paint ran in swirls, not taut between numbers. These saturating flowing colours where Old Angel hid his own belief made his brain feel intelligent; it must be so even to attempt to live with unproof. And so the small man feels big because he is friends with God.

Old Angel attempted to turn the world into an imaginary place, a place where nothing mattered except his own feelings and the understanding of them. Materialism came to mean more to him than simply the acquisition of goods and wealth. Materialism was the epitome of reality, of the tangibility of steel. Old Angel began to construct a world where real people mixed freely with those he imagined. In the corridors of his mind ghosts and angels jostled for space with people he knew and had met in the material world. In this place of imaginary beings God was easy to see. God would not, could not, leave a place that didn't exist.

Birmingham was the last place Old Angel and Victoria were grounded, as they had been on their wedding day. Here their flying began, the twenty-year ascent of marriage which it is not possible to call, by turning turbulence into, poetry. Birmingham was loud enough to muffle the sound of their vows. Its steam and clatter also covered the mistake they had made. When Joyce had warned Victoria about Old Angel's sulking, Victoria had ignored the warning. Her mistake had been to believe she knew Old Angel better than his mother. As soon as they had their own house together he treated her as he had treated his mother. She was of course, in many ways, merely a substitute. Old Angel found another armchair and ignored Victoria from it. This was the beginning of twenty years, but when Old Angel became a minister and they left Birmingham to return to Nottingham it was too late for friendship; they had become strangers.

And strange breeds strange. Victoria and Old Angel produced two sons in Nottingham. Two boys who were the product of two people unable to love one another. It is only to be expected that the two boys would descend into the shadows of weirdness lit by candles, that they would join the shelter for the weak: Tigguacobaucc. The house, with this family in it, sat south of the Trent in an area of Nottingham called West Bridgford. But love, though strange, was not absent. The house was halfway along Pierrepont Road, settled and semi-detached. Some might say that this road is in Lady Bay, not Bridgford, but only those who care. There was no love from parent to parent, and only a tiny portion from father to sons, but from the mother to her boys love flowed incessant.

And the size of things is what youth is all about.

Old Angel was a good minister. His sermons made old ladies jump in their seats, stood hair on the arms of strong men, terrified and delighted children. The strange and complex world of his own belief was portrayed to the congregation as simple and secure. But complexity waits like a lion in the grass, waiting to pounce and rip. He was so brilliant and exciting and safe up there in the pulpit, jacket off, walking easily around, shouting then whispering. He put into practice all he'd learnt from Burton, from his own father.

On stage he was a real father.

Then it happened. He fell in love for the second time. It was his nose that got him. It trapped his heart and his brain as though caught in metal teeth. He was gashed by smell. He could not repel it because it was not repellent. This was the first time a woman had taken control of him. She did not serve him and she would not do his bidding. She was approximately his height and he could not look down on her. Old Angel fell for someone who dominated (a common thing), who was proud of her smell (an uncommon thing). Victoria smelt her first. She knew another woman had entered her territory. Women are equally as territorial as men, and their senses sing at a higher pitch. But Old Angel soon could see nothing but smell (another uncommon thing).

This was the eighth malady.

It only took time for the woman to coat him with her scent, and for him to enjoy it. From the moment he first smelt her, Old Angel had no intention of staying with his two sons and Victoria. This is not to say that leaving was easy. It was not. He sat in the front room of the house on Pierrepont Road the night before he left. He had just given a sermon concerning the sanctity of marriage, and the irony of what he thought he might do played loudly in his head. The sound got louder until it became almost unbearable and he called out. It was proof, he decided, that his faith in God was finished.

Old Angel looked out of the front windows of his house at the stars. He was in pain but he knew the distance this star had travelled to prick him, he believed the science of light and speed were trying to wake him up. He was stroked by physics. But he did not believe that science could save him. It could show him his body at molecular level but his emotion had no molecules. Science could not give him advice.

He turned his head upwards and called out. Old Angel had not planned to call for anything in particular—what would be the point of calling to a random universe? But when his call became words, he was calling a demon. This is when he was sure his faith was dead. This was also the moment when Old Angel found that all good stories are invention and truth. Old Angel saw Orange Boy flutter onto the windowsill and come in to sit on Old Angel's shoulder. They talked quietly for hours until Orange Boy considered he had heard enough and gave Old Angel some advice. He suggested that Old Angel run far away to be with the woman whose skin smelt so strongly. The wise demon said of Old Angel and Victoria that in this world only one dead object could be brought to life. Orange Boy told Old Angel that though books are inanimate, under the correct conditions they have life, they will respond to palpation. It requires only the electricity running from the fingers of a sensitive reader to restart the phloem that was once their constitution. Old Angel listened as he was told that no matter where he decided to go, that place would not be enough for him. Orange Boy told him he should give Victoria time to find someone else, perhaps a man who enjoyed cliffs as she did, but once that had happened Old Angel must return to Nottingham. He would suffocate out there. There would be no magic.

Magic is the art of inventing the truth, but also of finding it.

Before he left Pierrepont Road Old Angel drew up a letter telling Victoria he had suffered and had made her suffer and had left. He went where the sea was strong and the ground free of caves. There is nothing to tell of his time there because Old Angel has not told me of it. But Old Angel has followed the advice of Orange Boy and has returned to Nottingham. He and I spend much time together in the caves. He enjoys listening and I enjoy talking, and as he also enjoys a constant pipe we are made for each other. I am used to his little habits. He keeps his hand on his heart and his ear to the roof of the cave. He is sure vibrations will be the death of us all.

Old Angel is a reader of books. He loves their life. He thinks that if I tell the stories of my friends, if I make them into a book, then I will find my own life, my own story. Yesterday he asked me what I thought of flowers; did I remember his philosophy on the reason for the existence of the earth? I told him he had never mentioned it before, but he shook his head. Old Angel told me not to worry—a demon once taught him books can bring the dead to life—and that I should continue. I must continue just the way I am, telling stories. He is a good friend.

chapter

the story of jalland

JALLAND. Jalland. Jalland. You are a friend, but I cannot slip you away from your crawl under so many influences. I know your body is safe, but your mind Jalland, your mind is not strong. I have watched you in the caves, seen you washing yourself with these bonds, seen in your eyes the names of drugs. What will you do next Jalland? When you have crawled above and below an entire city where is left to crawl? I know you do not care. I know you are a minion to your drugs. I know I care. Your drugs. What can be done with drugs that mean you no harm though they harm you? Let us begin with the names. Black Boy. Corner Pin. Hickling Laing. Drury. Rouse. Old Angel. Whiston. Plumtre. Drugs that mean you no harm. Drugs that love you.

Jalland is sick and he needs help. He needs to return to Sherwood Forest where he can flit amongst the leaves. This is not as simple as it sounds. He could drink the nectar of one hundred flowers to give him strength, then fly as fast as his tiny wings would carry him up Mansfield Road. He could. He would. He cannot. We are holding him here, influencing him, and Jalland is small but good. He will not desert us even if our needs kill him. It is well known that everyone needs someone to look after them, to disperse magic and lightness into their lives. It is also known that fairies bring a lightness beyond the reach of any other creature. This is what Jalland brings to us. Lightness. His body is a three inch sparkle in the caves. His command is our wish. His delicate wings flutter and brrr. Jalland brings much to Tigguacobaucc, but Tigguacobaucc has brought Jalland to his knees.

Jalland dances for his own enjoyment but also for the benefit of us, his friends. He dances every night all over Nottingham and in the morning ordinary people wake to find rings on their lawns. These circles of flattened grass are where Jalland has danced on the spot. Of course it is not only Jalland who dances, there are many fairies who come to the aid of the big people during the night, who come to watch over them. I have it from Jalland's own tiny honest mouth that fairy dances once took place over all of England. His mouth has also said that fairies now only dance in Nottingham. Nowhere else has the magic to sustain them. What city is this? Nottingham. Why is it famous? For many reasons. What does it hide? Only dancing fairies flattening the grass.

An invention and a truth.

It is well known that fairies beat rings onto grass with their tiny feet. It is not well known that these rings are their prisons as well as their ballrooms. Fairy Rings are The Rings for fairies. If big people were not so desperate and selfish, we might realise that fairies are held in their Rings by our lonely wishes. And if we wished for them to stop dancing and fly to Sherwood they would, because our wish is their command. But it is more usually the case that big people put their own problems before the health of fairies. Black Boy, Corner Pin, Hickling Laing, Rouse, Old Angel, Whiston, Plumtre. And me of course, and me. My name is Tigguacobaucc and I am as guilty as anyone for entrapping fairies, for holding Jalland under my influence.

Jalland came to Tigguacobaucc under his own influence first; we did not call him. We would gradually come together more often in the mine that Rouse has spent his life digging, and talk of what brought us here. Of what drove us underground. Our lives became stories and those stories became art. Tigguacobaucc is the gallery for that work. In those early days of our talk, Jalland would sit on someone's hand and listen, or perhaps hover near the sandy ceiling to get an aerial view of our difficulties. He was not capable of providing answers, or of giving advice like Orange Boy. Jalland is not a demon and so does not possess the wisdom of one. But he is a fairy and wishes will pass through him if the wish is right and true for the person requesting it. Jalland cannot make magic happen, though it happens through him. So far he has helped almost everyone.

Jalland heard Black Boy crying out for faith. He knew that Orange Boy would give good advice, and that Black Boy would build a heart in his living room. He knew that a heart could give Black Boy strength but not wonder. And it is wonder that is a fairy speciality. However hard they try, demons cannot impart it. Wisdom and wonder go hand in hand but are never drawn from the same source. It was Jalland who filled the abscess left in Black Boy by faith. He touched Black Boy's head and made him think of trees in a way he never thought possible. The energy of Black Boy that night along Trent Bridge was an energy given to him by a good fairy. I remember that night again.

Black Boy became animated and his long eyes were wide with energy. He forgot the heart for the first time in weeks, pulling his fingers down the crocodilian bark. He held his nose against the girth and smelt this giant. Inside, he said, were rings, but unlike The Rings that made us suffer, these rings shot nourishment through the height of the tree to its leaves. Black Boy described the life of trees as immeasurably slow stretches. From underground each new plant would push to the surface, then over many of our lifetimes it would reach for the sun.

We cannot follow the progress of an individual because we lack time. To chart one tree means passing its location to another human who will return years after us and glimpse, only to pass to another person and another. The individual grows further out of reach and wider, charting in rings within its body. Death will come eventually as with all life, but if left untouched an individual makes a mockery of our centuries. Black Boy told me of Major Oak in Sherwood Forest who has almost lived for a millennium. Black Boy spoke with the conviction of the converted. He did not know until now that Jalland had filled his head with a love of trees normally associated with only the gentlest fairies. It satisfies them as it satisfies Black Boy.

Underground, Jalland keeps an eye on the speeding Corner Pin. Unlike Orange Boy he can easily keep up with him and often flies before Corner Pin's pained eyes, lighting his run through the labyrinth with his sparkling wings. Jalland can do little for Corner Pin except keep him from crashing. This in itself is a big enough job for any fairy.

Corner Pin had been special to Jalland ever since he was a child. Jalland recognised something in Corner Pin that made him stick with him. He saw that Corner Pin felt safe when he made himself small, when he curled his body into itself. Jalland had flown in the bedroom window many nights when Corner Pin would wake screaming. Jalland knew that Corner Pin was dreaming of uncertainty, and that the fear of it would throw him awake. His mother hid the suffering inflicted upon her by the father, but like many children, Corner Pin was registering his mother's unhappiness without intention. Corner Pin always was a creature of premonition. He never dreamt images, only what he later called rhythms, and even later, observed during his life in Tigguacobaucc, The Rings. In some ways people believed him to be blessed from God, especially those in the church. But most who are blessed in the eyes of others are damned in their own. His ability not to see but to *feel* into the future would eventually send him underground. Running underground at speed, as he does now, pushes pain through his legs like an injected drug through the blood. It hurts him. But his premonitory Rings haunted him even in the tainted idyll of his childhood. Those legs, which would later rush him beneath Nottingham, would wake him in agony.

And on hearing the sound, Jalland would appear on the pillow and the hum of his wings would calm Corner Pin. Jalland would sit beside the head of Corner Pin, glinting like a tiny guiding star and whispering into his ear. In a minutely magical way Corner Pin, like Black Boy and Old Angel, was stroked by physics. After calming Corner Pin in this way, Jalland would fly out to the huge garden and dance rings for him. His tiny feet would spin and twirl him in a desperate energy, desperate because he wanted to bring as much lightness into Corner Pin's life before his father left. Jalland knew why Corner Pin's legs were preparing him to run, and he had promised to follow him as he gathered speed.

You may have wondered how Corner Pin can run with such swiftness through a pitch black labyrinth without crashing. It is a good question, though it is your own choice whether or not to believe the answer. Corner Pin does not crash because he is not in total darkness. Just enough light is brought into his life to enable him to survive life at high speed, and the light sparkles from a tiny creature buzzing behind his ear. Jalland. Jalland. Jalland. Stay with Corner Pin my friend, you are the only one fast enough to protect him.

The story of Jalland is one with a message split into many messages. Sprites exist just as God exists, but not as most of us believe. Is it not possible that a storyteller writing of a period in history may stumble upon truth by inventing it, just as the historian stumbles upon truth if he works one place for his whole life? So far so linear. The storyteller may embolden the past with many realities, with details physical or imagined. Such details invented by the storyteller are the nuggets professional historians sift for, spending entire careers watching for one piece of information that may bring to life a period or person. Storytellers are no less professional but are not bound by the need to recover definite facts; instead they can invent.

The historian and the storyteller are both creating pictures. That the storyteller's picture may or may not be true is of no consequence. If historians stumble upon evidence by chance, is it not possible that also by chance the storyteller's details may be true? Humans cannot for the most part decide what is left visible by history. That which cannot be found must be invented. The invention may be a truth. The storyteller, the inventor of a character, may have stumbled upon the real story of someone dead for centuries, neglected due to unimportance or embarrassment. It is written that two monks lived in the caves of Lenton Hermitage in 1244. It is not written that they were in love.

The truth of history is nothing but a small glitter in the sand, a roll of dice, a story.

Jalland has not been visible to many of those he dances for, but Hickling Laing could always see him as clearly as he could see God. However, as was the case with Drury, Hickling Laing did not for a time appreciate what fluttered beside him. He knew Jalland was a fairy but did not realise that Jalland's presence was enabling him to be happy. In all the lonely times of his childhood before the appearance of Drury, Hickling Laing was still happy. And Jalland danced in his garden. When Hickling Laing stood looking over Nottingham from Mapperley Top, it was Jalland giving him a sense of joy. And Jalland danced in his garden. It was Jalland who suggested that Drury might have at last found a safe friend when he heard of a boy who'd been born with jet black eyes. And Jalland danced in his garden. Jalland's tiny wings glinted in the moonlight while Hickling Laing read book after book and learned the dogma of disbelief. And Jalland danced in his garden all through the stories of all of us, growing weaker by the night.

Jalland has never helped Drury. There is little between them. Jalland can fly fast but is not able to avoid the glare of Drury, who can of course be in all places at once, though it takes a lot out of him. For much of the time theirs is a finagling relationship, though Drury always has the upper hand. Jalland has the same attitude towards Drury as all imaginary beings do. He is scared of him. Drury hates the fact that because of the nature of his position other imaginary beings feel inclined to avoid him. God has always admired fairies for their devotion to big people. A devotion he personally never thought worth it until he fell in love with Car. God knows that fairies feel threatened almost constantly. Their home in Sherwood Forest is getting smaller, and many of them are having to find leaves in Nottingham to keep them warm while they sleep. This is not pleasant, for Nottingham may be unusual in its magic but it is common in its noise.

Jalland deals with God mainly through craftiness and trickery. This is the way all fairies deal with Drury. They are under the same misimpression that ordinary humans suffer: that God is an all powerful and revengeful being. We now know that this is not true. We know that God has fallen in love with something that will die. We also know that God is powerless to save Car, to save his own saviour.

What does this say about our conception of God?

Exaggeration comes in many forms and in all of them it is an underrated virtue. And surely the highest form of exaggeration is the fairytale. We suffer misconceptions of fairies too. It is true they are small. It is true they fly on glittering wings. It is true that sneezing endangers their lives. It is true they wrap themselves in leaves to sleep. It is true they dance on grass. It is not true that they fear and hate humans. It is true they will sacrifice their own happiness for the happiness of the big people who are their influences, their drugs. It is not true they are substantial forever.

Rouse therefore has been watched by a series of fairies. He is like one of Black Boy's beloved trees because he has lived for too long to be watched by a single fairy. They pass him on to one another as a special case. Not one has been able to bring true happiness and magic into his life, though it was Jalland who conversed with the ghost of Robin Hood. He told Robin that a man who could not stop digging had been inspired by his final arrow, and that Rouse had chosen a resting place for his wife in the same way. Robin believed the story of the lonely miner and sank further underground to find him. Jalland sometimes goes down to visit Rouse, and listens to the finest archer England has ever seen talking freely to a man obsessed with sand. On these nights, then, a silvery fairy hangs in the air between a two hundred year old man and Robin Hood.

What does this say about our understanding of myth and legend?

Old Angel only began to know of Jalland when he returned from the sea. When Old Angel lived on Pierrepont Road he wanted nothing to do with fairies. They were stories for children, flippant and without substance. He suffered the usual human problem of perspective—how could something so small be important? Old Angel now knows that fairies are some of the strongest and most honourable beings living in Nottingham. Old Angel changed near the sea; he felt its tug and throw as deep as the beat of his own heart. It made him understand that all things are connected. Blood may be thicker than water but it exists for the same reason—to carry life onwards.

In his new house by the sea, he threw away childish acceptance and became a questioning man. His garden was his laboratory and his plants experiments. But he grew no fruit. This garden was many times smaller than the one he had left in Nottingham. Instead of harvesting and thanking God for his goodness he learned to fill the garden with flowers. They were of no use. They could not be eaten. They appeared only for a short time. They required a higher level of patience. He grew them only for the sake of their beauty, and so he stumbled upon the reason for the existence of the earth—that there was no reason for its existence.

When Old Angel did return to Nottingham on Orange Boy's advice, he found that advice to be true. Old Angel had started to suffocate away from Nottingham. There had not been enough magic to sustain him. It is for the same reason that all of England's fairies now dance in Nottingham. And in their dance is invention and art. They throw light on the lives in whose gardens they dance, and like all magicians will sometimes trip on new truth. The truth that fairies uncover in their wild movements is often a different angle for their charges to view life. By ancient tiny magic they suck answers from the earth through their feet, then fly into the bedrooms of big people and whisper them into sleeping minds.

Fairy whispers are often called dreams by those who live in Nottingham.

When Old Angel began to grow only flowers in his garden he was stepping in the right direction. He was moving away from ignorance of the physical world to stand in wonder before it. He understood, as Drury would confirm, that the world is not moving to some great plan, to a grand purpose. It is an exploiter of chance. The earth made its first exploitation when the correct chemicals existed in the correct atmosphere. Life bubbled and ever since then all creatures have developed as opportunists. Fairies are no exception.

Old Angel has recently discovered a flaw in his philosophy on flowers. For many years he had believed flowers to be beautiful but useless except for their own reproduction. But a few nights ago he sat in his new garden in Nottingham. It was early evening and silence was suspended in a pink yellow sky. Old Angel relaxed but he could hear a small sound coming from one of his flower beds. He listened more carefully and moved his ears close to the flowers. These are ears obsessed with tiny vibrations, ready to brace for the vibration that will kill, but this sound did not get louder. It was coming from a red red tulip. Old Angel peered inside, and there, resting its silver head against the stamen, was a fairy. From that evening Old Angel decided never to cut flowers for his house.

Any flower in any garden may give comfort to a fairy, tired from dancing magic and lightness into the lives of big people.

Jalland has helped Whiston. He spends some nights with him on Canning Circus, watching him try to make his mind up. Whiston enjoys the company of Jalland and he knows that Jalland brings silver light into his life. The decision to stand in the centre of the Circus and allow life to spin around him, or to find a seat on the edge is a decision which can fill whole hours of Whiston's life. He is not sick but he does have too much time on his hands.

Plumtre is very rich. Like Old Angel, he has seen fairies in his garden, and it is a garden containing dangerous beasts. Plumtre is the only one among my friends who can afford to live in The Park estate: hundreds of beautiful houses lying in the shadow of the castle. It is beneath Plumtre's garden that lions sit cold as stone. They would be killers if magic could release them from the cave wall that holds them.

In the Lace Market Jalland has his own cave. He goes there when he needs to be alone. His cave is under the north side of Goose Gate on Heathcoat Street.

It is beneath a pub. Jalland's cave is really a series of wine vaults. Under the busy pub there are rooms, stairs, wells and a lift shaft, all cut into the sandstone. He rests there after giving his all to some poor creature in a dance. He lies on a bed of dried flowers in the dark when all his light has been sacrificed.

Most of the beings, ordinary or imaginary, that know of Tigguacobaucc have somewhere to themselves other than Rouse's labyrinth. When an entire underground city is accessible it is easy to find your own shadows. Jalland is not a martyr. He does not dance purely for the benefit of big people. Fairies are like scavenger fish, devoted to cleaning the sharp skin of sharks. They hold to the bodies of huge predators providing a service, but at the same time satisfying their own hunger. It is a dangerous job but they enjoy it. Fairies clean the lives of big people, give them dreams, dance for them. But dancing is food to a fairy, they cannot live without it and so benefit by the service they provide. Fairies enjoy their job but it is dangerous.

It is well known that many fairies have died from exhaustion. They possess an enthusiasm that can outmanoeuvre their common sense. Once fairies start dancing they find it almost impossible to stop. Jalland is more than an exponent of these facts, he is the greatest example of them. Jalland dances for more big people than any other fairy in Nottingham, and those big people agreed that it would only be a matter of time before the little fairy collapsed and became a tiny silver statistic. We should have all spoken to him and asked him to stop dancing for us but we could not. We have spoken of Jalland when he has been resting in his own cave and agreed that one fine day we might all become responsible for his death. We know that he and his fairy troupe are in Nottingham because they feel safe here, that there is magic enough to sustain their magical existence. All of us realise that we are following the example of the earth in our exploitation of the powers of our fairy friend. None of us has the courage to cease the dancing of this fairy; it would mean the end of so much lightness, the end of good dreams.

What does this say about the quality of our own dreams?

Jalland and all the fairies in Nottingham are caught in the tragedy of their own purpose. If they do not stop dancing for the dreams of big people they will drive themselves into tiny graves. Jalland himself is already on his knees for us. But equally, if they do stop dancing, the whole drive of their fairy lives will come to a halt. They will be unable to feel happiness because they would not be whispering it to others. To dance or not to dance? That is the question. If only William Shakespeare could himself be questioned. It is well known that he understood the minds and hearts of fairies. Perhaps he could be persuaded to part with some advice on what these remaining creatures should do. If, as it seems, God in love, an orange demon, a librarian who does not know who he is, a fairy, an angered ancient man and Robin Hood are all seated here against the sandy walls of Tigguacobaucc, is it not possible that William Shakespeare might sit himself down with us to answer a few of his own questions? Which of these are inventions and which truths?

Magic is the art of inventing the truth, but also of finding it.

Old Angel, our reader of books, has told me that in the rhymes of *A Midsummer Night's Dream* there lies help. That in William Shakespeare's play of dreams and woods and fairies is aid to the problems of the fairies of Nottingham. Hickling Laing read all of Shakespeare while he rested his elbows on the high wooden arms of the red chair, and he has agreed that if help lies anywhere it is amongst the pages of that dreaming.

When dreams lose harmony they become nightmares.

Jalland has spent more of his time with me since I returned to Nottingham than with anyone else. This is not something I am proud of because it is my Rings which are causing the problems. It is the circle in which I find myself trapped that is draining the energy of Jalland. It will be my fault if he falls to the ground on broken wings because I am so complicated, so involved. I cannot seem to make my life simple, to let it run smoothly. My name is Tigguacobaucc and yet I have no name. Someone who says he loves me and regrets what he did to me told me to take that name. Tigguacobaucc. A person and a place. An invention and a truth. I am forced to watch Jalland dance magic into my life because it is in his nature to dance. I cannot free him from my influence because I am scared to let go of his tiny hand; all of us are the same. How can someone so small be so important? Very easily.

The story of Jalland's family is short—there is no family. Like all fairies Jalland sprang from a flower, and again like all fairies he will smell of that birthplace all his life. Jalland leaves the scent of white roses in his wake. Jalland never knew his parents even though they did exist. All fairies refer to one another as brother and sister, so it is easy for them to become incestuous and produce offspring with a fairy who might be their own mother or father. These couplings are of no concern to fairies and never have been. Little people do not tie themselves with the regulations of big people.

So Jalland has only ever flown with brothers and sisters, and though none can be sure, most of them probably are true siblings. This creates unbreakable bonds amongst fairies and arguments are rare and quickly resolved. Jalland has always danced in Sherwood Forest and Nottingham, but he can no longer manage both. His wings do not have the power to carry him to Sherwood after he has danced for me, so he usually just collapses in my garden. He has met all of the people whose stories are being told to free my own story from its Rings. They all understand that in his tiny way Jalland is essential to that quest. After all, what is a story without magic and exaggeration? The story of my life runs on both fuels.

I should take hold of myself by the neck and tell Jalland to stop dancing for me, to rest. I should do this and launch myself into a life without lightness and magic. I should. I cannot. My name is Tigguacobaucc and I do not have the courage to rid myself of fairies; they bring me to life. If I did not know what powers are wrenched from the earth by their tiny feet, I might more easily tell Jalland I do not need him. But I am versed in his magic and cannot save him by stopping him from saving me. Knowledge is not always appreciated. I have promised to guide you through the stories of my friends as well as I will through the twists and turns of Tigguacobaucc. I have told you I am stuck with loving. I have handed you tins of red paint to stripe the city with, to enjoy yourself. To be caught in the greatest city in the world, if only for the length of time it might take to read a book. To guzzle yourself full of Nottingham. I have warned you only to believe some of the words I pass before your eyes. I don't want to blind anyone.

Confusion can be very convincing. The story of Jalland is a story with many messages. One of those messages warns of disaster when control is lost and malevolent forces of nature gain an upper hand. Neither ordinary nor imaginary beings are protected against the chemistry in which they live and are made on. Old Angel told me what can be learnt from William Shakespeare's Dream. He said within earshot of Jalland that quick bright things can come to confusion. Old Angel told me of the antithesis between love and reason—he called this antithesis 'adolescent whirl'. A less harmful version of The Rings. He said he could see that I was in love but that these were dangerous times for me. I did not even know who I was. Could I possibly be under a spell, an illusion that I simply called love—and am I mistaking this illusion for reality? Old Angel thinks that I might be uncomfortable in a world of illusion. He has suggested that when I entered it I lost track of what had been reality. This reality took many forms: my family, my city, my name.

I have lost all of these things. But what have I gained? Invention through truth. If I free myself from The Rings will I be left with a dull life without magic? Will I forget Drury as easily as I once forgot myself? Jalland. Jalland. Jalland. What about love? I am beginning to think that this life of invention is the truer one, the less painful. I feel stuck between one Nottingham of the linear day-to-day, and another Nottingham of anti-linear magic. The Rings may hurt me and hold me and harm my tiny friend Jalland, but they are so real in their illusions. So free in their bonds.

These stories are not persiflage even though they might entertain. They are written for the purpose of finding a single story. Old Angel calls them a way to come out of a wood of dreams more mature than when I went in. He says that maturity is the ability to accept things you would not previously have accepted. In the case of these stories it is that the ordinary world can be enriched by the world of the imagination. Illusions are essential as realities. But in a case as serious as my own and wide enough to encompass the whole of Nottingham, there is more to these illusions than might be apparent. Not everything I have told you is invention, is shadow.

"How shall we find the concord of this discord?"

Those words from the shadows, from the steps down into this labyrinth. Did you hear them too? Of course you did. They came loud from the Peel Street entrance. I suppose it is not unheard of for wishes to come true in Tigguacobaucc. I will continue as Old Angel has advised. Jalland is determined to survive the telling of his story. All fairies, all fairytales, remind us of the precarious nature of human happiness. This is due to the devotion and delicacy of fairies to the big people who need them. If we are mature enough to accept that fairies exist then we will see them. If we are this mature then our happiness stands a much stronger chance of survival. Happiness, especially in love, can only be achieved through an open imagination. If we do not imagine, then only part of our own stories are visible. We are not whole. I may have imagined too much and cannot distinguish realities. I have knowledge of too many stories and need to shed a few of their skins.

A person with no story is a diseased person. As is a person with too many.

But there I have done it again. I hijacked Jalland's story for my own ends just as I have everyone's. However, it is me making the effort to tell these things. You would probably not have known that fairies are endangered without these stories. Jalland must be helped. I understand the language of medicine but I am not skilled to practice what I preach. Though Jalland requires more than a doctor. His condition is a common one for people in Tigguacobaucc. He has problems with his heart. Anyway, what would a doctor for big people be able to do for a heart as small and weak as Jalland's?

"Love can transpose to form and dignity."

There is the voice again, louder still. It is accompanied by wind, the same wind that Robin Hood pushes before him when he moves. I can feel on my face the wind that ghosts make. On the backs of my wrists the hairs are rising in apprehension of what may be around the corners of this tribute to Rouse's anger.

What Jalland needs is strength. He will not die if he drinks enough nectar. We have not the skill to lift him from his knees and suckle him. What Jalland needs is love. His form will transpose and become substantial if he can be kissed by another fairy. There are none unattached in Nottingham. What Jalland needs is dignity. He must be shown the famous of his tiny race. He will dance with new grace when he meets his honoured brothers and sisters. Jalland has spent many evenings dancing dreams into my head. His feet have always been at one with his body. He has not missed a step. I will know a kind of happiness as long as Jalland lives. Jalland will live if he can maintain harmony in his steps, if he can dance the tightrope between despair and joy. Jalland must do what all fairies are called to do. He must find the concord of his discord, for when dreams lose their harmony they become nightmares. What Jalland needs is guidance. He is suffering under us. We are influences beyond his control, drugs that harm him. He can be seen crawling under the weight of our problems, exhausted from dancing to throw new light on our difficulties. Nottingham is the last home of fairies and I am worried that it might become their grave. Jalland and his fairy friends need the hand of an expert. This is more likely to happen in Nottingham than anywhere else.

Jalland is too courageous to leave us without his magic and we are too without courage to ask him to do so. It is well known that fairies sparkle and fly. It is less well known they do so for our benefit.

"But we are spirits of another sort."

And that voice is getting closer, beginning to find us by the light of our candles. Whoever it is must be made of some kind of magic himself, and it is a man's voice. I can hear it. We all can. It is a strong Midlands accent of authority, but also humour. If these things can be deciphered by the diapason of vocal chords, then I would say we are hearing from the shadows the double voice of comedy and tragedy. It walks the tightrope asked of fairies, but it is not the voice of a fairy. It is too expansive. It is a voice that is making Jalland sit up from his exhaustion. He is not speaking even though he has begun to smile.

"Every elf and fairy sprite
  Hop as light as bird from brier:
And this ditty, after me,
Sing, and dance it trippingly."

You can hear the voices too. There is more than one now, though he is still leading. And someone is beating rhythms on the skin of a drum. I can hear dancing. Look, Jalland is beating his wings for the first time this evening. He has barely moved for all the other stories. His tiny body looked as though it might be absorbed into the sand any minute. His pointed ears did not even perk for his own story. The others have all been listening carefully to me, watching for inaccuracies, waiting to see if I emerge from the chrysalistic state of their stories into the many-coloured entity of my own.

Jalland. Jalland. Jalland. Look at him now. He is fluttering with energy I thought had left him. He is trying to tell me something... come and whisper into my ear Jalland, conserve yourself. There are new shadows rounding that pillar behind us; the singers and shouters and drummers are nearly with us.

"If we shadows have offended,"

Well, I can hardly hear what this fairy is telling me...

"Think but this, and all is mended—"

Jalland my friend, say that again... he says ghosts of the most famous fairies in the world are coming. He tells me quietly, they are bringing the only big person who understood them, who knew fairies without becoming their drug. Jalland says that because he himself is a fairy wishes can pass through him and come true. I have wished for him to stay alive. I cannot yet rid him of my influence.

And here are the fairies dancing... Oberon Titania Puck Peaseblossom Cobweb Moth Mustardseed... flitting round William Shakespeare who offers Jalland orange nectar, a smile across his double face.

chapter 8

the story of whiston

CANNING Circus spins in its day and night spin, releasing life in Nottingham. Anything could happen here and anything does. It is a place of costume and trickery, a pantomime parietal containing the functions that make it a circus for the greatest city in the world. On their edges, scared and confused sit talking to themselves on the edge. In the centre magic players compete in pubs for speed of hand and blink of eye. Lives pitch their frequencies into the fine junk heart and lung mish-mash. Canning Circus, somewhere found for the lost. Air and love. The necessary. Anything could happen here and anything does.

Shaped unlike a circle it is circular. Without a big top it is still a circus. It is the ring for a repine master and is replete with lions in its wings. I am almost too late to be its storyteller; imagination has already run riot around it. But, as Old Angel has said, I must continue as I am, telling stories; and this is the story of Whiston, the fretful master of Canning Circus. Whiston spends hours trying to decide whether to sit on the edge in safety or go into the centre and let life spin around him. Whiston's mind is constantly made up. He is the opposite of indecisive and the antithesis to hesitation. But he is the mirror image of whatever direction he has at any moment decided to take. Whiston is the reflection of Whiston, reversed and confused.

He is like this because he has been nowhere else. He was born in a large flat on the island of buildings in the centre of the circus. It came as no surprise to him when many years later he found himself the Ringmaster. Some posts in Nottingham need to be explained. The Sheriff of Nottingham is no longer a vile despot, though holders often feel this history in their blood. The Sheriff has no cause to pursue Robin, though it has not been common knowledge that he can still be chased. The Ringmaster of Canning Circus is an almost unknown position and Whiston is not inclined to brag about it. He might do so were he any good at the job, but sadly this is not the case.

Whiston's grip on magic is that he can see clearly what Canning Circus is: an answer. His grip, though, is loose. It is strange that the man who lives where The Rings fear to tread is caught by that place. Canning Circus will not let him go.

Whiston fell from between his mother's legs like an omelette, yellow and folded. He has been sick all of his life, so has never had the energy to pull his jaundiced body out of the Circus. It is here with the cars and costumes that he has had his life. It is here that he will go underground for the final time. Going underground has been Whiston's only time away. He is here with the rest of us in Tigguacobaucc, waiting for something to happen. He has watched anything happen many times except the one happening he hopes for. Whiston is not unusual in his hope, for he hopes one fine day to be set free.

Going underground.

On one curve of Canning Circus is Canning Terrace; you saw it before I began my stories. Canning Terrace is a row of white houses standing like a great cake at the gates of a cemetery sweeping down from the Circus. The houses all have green doors. In the centre of the Terrace is a wide archway through which it is possible to see the gravestones. Above the archway is a clock, the hands inveterate in their journey. The clock is believed by most people in Nottingham to mark time until they pass through the archway into their grave and lie down for the last time. But, as some of my friends' stories warn, this is often not true. Not everyone is eternally still.

Though going underground can be final, there are those who never get up to stretch their legs. In Nottingham of course, going underground is common. Tigguacobaucc sends us deeper than six feet under. Down here anything can happen, and looking over the faces of my audience I can see that anything does. I have found that going underground is the finest way to fight The Rings, or at least avoid them. The Rings. Depression. The Rings. A great loss. All of us have lost important things. My name is Tigguacobaucc but the air is clearing around that mouthful. My brain is jolting and giving me information that has fallen too fast for me to catch, too deep for retrieval. So far I clutch a clue. I remember my name was once very short and easy to remember, if only I could. And if I could, everything else would be within reach. Information storage and retrieval. These are words of my profession. I am a librarian, an expert in organising. I am used to millions of bits and pieces because that is what libraries are. A librarian will balance the need for everything to be seen but also for it to be tidy. Librarians are anti-minimalists, they cannot live without clutter so they have developed ways to live with it.

The air is clearing. Air and love. The necessary. At least I can feel one of these on my face.

Whiston is constantly his own opposite. He always knows what to do but never does it because he always knows the alternative. He is at the extreme of alternative lifestyles. For instance, the graves. Whiston looks through Canning Terrace archway at the upright stones with a light heart. He is not afraid of the day his eyes will finally close on Canning Circus and his body is carried beneath the clock to be dropped flat in a hole. He imagines the scene and encourages the thought that life will stop spinning around him. But. But. In the absence of fear lies his fear. Whiston looks at the graves and wants to live. He urges the blood to be pumped stronger through his heart, hearing its beat. He can feel his white cells battling to keep his eyes open. He holds his hands in front of his face and in wonder moves each finger down and up. Deliberate. Amazed at his ability to make these small things happen. He adores the idea that burial will release him from Canning Circus, but knows that this would mean paralysis. Whiston would no longer have the skill to order his fingers about. His heart pushes the blood into battle and wins to fight another day. He decides to die. He decides to live.

The cruelty of The Rings. To make a man live in Canning Circus, where The Rings can be released and yet trap him there. Old Angel has told me that Canning Circus is a place of conclusion and of beginning. Everyone suffers under The Rings. All of us need to finish what we cannot and start what seems impossible. Jalland would call this our dream, and his folk should know.

As it was with Black Boy, the first time I met Whiston was in my library. He had spent the afternoon in hospital being tested and told he suffered from Gilbert's Syndrome. Whiston spoke at great length to the doctor but decided he needed more information, so he came to me. I found him what he wanted. I am sure he will not mind if I go into his medical condition in some detail; I am after all a storyteller. Gilbert's Syndrome is an inherited metabolic disorder leading to increased unconjugated hyperbilirubinæmia. The condition begins shortly after birth and is an inborn failure to uptake bilirubin, which is formed from the breakdown of hæmoglobin. It is usually conjugated by all hepatocytes, but in Gilbert's Syndrome some may remain unconjugated and move in the circulation. Jaundice occurs during intercurrent illness, and as Whiston is almost always in a state of sickness he still looks like an omelette.

From this position of medical and mental weakness Whiston attempts to be the ringmaster of Canning Circus. It does not surprise anyone that for many years Canning Circus has lost battles to The Rings. Let me tell you what Drury has told me.

One thousand years ago, when Nottingham was entirely underground, it was called Tigguacobaucc, meaning 'Place of Caves'. Tigguacobaucc was an outcrop of rock surrounded by rich forest, trees whose ancestors would be the most famous forest in the world: Sherwood. In those days the sun was strong on the hairy backs of hunting men as they chased animals through the dapple for food. In the cool shelter of caves women sat rubbing sticks and painting the walls. They had children who were taught according to their sex. Girls sat beside their mothers and learnt delicate skills, while the boys rode amongst the hair of their father's backs, catching with keen eyes how to catch meat.

These people believed that the most fertile ground produces most riches. In this logic they were not simple but at the same time not lost. They had logic but there was no argument and so they did not suffer confusion. Situations did not run in circles and The Rings could not exist without complexity.

Occasionally there would be one or two among them who became bored with a life of routine. Each day was the same except for a backdrop of weather.

The restless would venture far into the forest and return months, even years later with stories. Between them these travellers walked until the sea halted them in all four directions and from this they concluded that their forest was in the middle of a massive island. This made all of Tigguacobaucc feel safe. Not only were they protected by water, and not only did a forest hide them, but they found the sandstone easy to carve into deep homes.

One thousand years is not a long time, but Nottingham has always been a place where anything can happen. These people knew about many things. They knew how to construct wood into useful objects and that fire can both feed and destroy. They were organised. The hunting parties were not random charges and the painting was not slap-dash. Like all societies Tigguacobaucc had its own sophistication, and its people celebrated in ways that seemed appropriate.

The conurbation of caves jutted above the trees. Centuries later, this would be where the Sheriff of Nottingham planned to chase an animal called Robin Hood between the trunks of his great forest. An invention and a truth. There was no castle in Tigguacobaucc, but its people could walk above the tree line to another high place. Here they performed their ceremonies and they called it The Circus. These words are lost but I have an eyewitness. Drury has seen Nottingham in all its states. The people of Tigguacobaucc believed in many things but Drury was not one of them; even then steeples did not rise over the trees. The Circus was a place where routine could be forgotten. During the day the women came to sit there and think about who they were. Some felt content with a simple life of caring for the men who provided for them, a life spent chattering about small things. Others secretly dreamed of joining the travellers who told stories about the breadth of their island, travellers who were all male. And in the evening these men would gather to boast of their skill in catching the creatures of the forest.

The Circus was a large flat space chosen for its height. Humans have always tried to gain a bird's eye view of their lives, and the people of Tigguacobaucc learnt much about themselves up there. On the edge of the circle there were seats made from wood. Some people lacked the confidence to approach the centre and would just sit, spectating. These people were often the less outgoing, the hurt, the confused. The others—the travellers, the storytellers, the hunters—were unafraid of effervescence. In the centre of The Circus was a kind of altar. It was not resplendent, for these were not rich people, but it was special. The altar was again made of wood and sat wide and tall at the centre of life in Tigguacobaucc. It looked like a high table and at each of its ends an object was placed. At one side a twig bent almost at a right angle, representing Air through trees blown by the wind. At the other side a wooden bowl with a lid. The bowl contained cutaneous remnants, dead skin from living partners representing Love. I am told by Drury that the people of Tigguacobaucc called their altar The Necessary.

The Necessary. An altar of two parts. An invention and a truth.

In those days everyone in Tigguacobaucc knew of The Circus and used it daily to replenish their lungs and hearts. They believed Air and Love to be the most important aspects necessary to sustain life. They understood that food and water and shelter were essential but did not rate them worthy of reflection; these things were too tangible. The people of Tigguacobaucc found themselves stimulated by the mysterious. They were interpreters of signs and accepted the normality of magic. Even then, if someone said they had seen a fairy dancing in the moonshine, everyone would nod and think how unlucky they had been not to have seen it. Exaggeration comes in many forms and in all of them it is an underrated virtue. In Tigguacobaucc, the fairytale has always been known as the strongest form of exaggeration.

In Tigguacobaucc the mysterious is anything that manifests itself differently in different people. Into this category fell and still falls: exaggerations fairies gods drugs landscapes air love stories. These are the things that have stimulated people in Nottingham long before the city ran over the forest. All of them are good. All of them are intangible and untamed, impossible to predict but with the potential to set free those who risk their major organs to experience such things.

A tradition was begun in Tigguacobaucc that The Circus required a Ringmaster to maintain it, but this was not a place of worship. The people did not believe in beings greater than themselves. The Circus was merely a place of reflection, somewhere to make links in life. Tigguacobaucc people knew their lives were held together by relationships and common experience, agreement and a mutual sense of place. If any magic really existed here it was that many different people could all feel it. Happiness was unusual on the great island but common in Tigguacobaucc. As with any society there were people on the edge, afraid to believe in themselves, though they were a minority. The Ringmaster had no choice about ascending to the job. He was picked from birth due to his yellow skin. The current Ringmaster would then bring the boy up, and as yellow skin was found to be hereditary it was always the boy's father. The Ringmasters present and future were always sick because of their disease. They were trapped by illness, caught by the tradition of The Circus, bound by the colour of their skin.

A generation would live without a Ringmaster if only girls were produced by the previous incumbent. The people of Tigguacobaucc decreed this to be the case, saying that only men had the strength required to harness the magic of The Circus. What they really meant was that a lifetime of cleaning and preparing The Circus for reflection should be work for sick males good for little else. Even in the most harmonious societies there are dishonest motives.

The training of a new Ringmaster revolved around acquiring skills to respect and understand reflection. It was the job of the Ringmaster to remind storytellers that one journey may contain many others hidden within its lines. He was to show by a lifetime of dedication to The Circus that, though his body was confined, his mind roamed free between the fabulous and the real. By his very presence the Ringmaster displayed the exact equality of mind and body. A mind could not function minus the other major organs, but equally, a body could have no rest and purpose without a mind of understanding and adventure. The Ringmaster was to maintain The Circus as a place of reflection, as somewhere the people of Tigguacobaucc could find answers to their problems by finding the undercurrents of their stories. Occasionally, someone who had lost their entire story might come to The Circus. There it may be possible for them to dig their own story from between the lines of the stories of friends and family.

An ancient town such as Tigguacobaucc gradually grows, and for Tigguacobaucc this meant onto the surface. This was the birth of Nottingham. As the town turned into a city it felled the forest like a huge ship cutting through a sea of trees. All of this took many centuries but Drury chronicled the lot. He had seen the people of Tigguacobaucc change, becoming always what they considered to be modern. He watched them throw off the past.

Drury also noticed that each year fewer and fewer people used The Circus as somewhere to make links in their lives. The stories of individuals became more substantial, less malleable. People stopped reflecting for long periods on their own stories. Even if they did spend time thinking about personal history, those thoughts grew more linear every year. The people of Tigguacobaucc and Nottingham—for now the two cities bunked together—were losing their ancient ability to see history as a floating random space. As they became more modern they became equally obsessed with facts. It is not necessary to interpret facts. They do not stand or fall on the deliberation of humans. They simply stand. It requires no flair to live a life of facts. As the people of Tigguacobaucc came increasingly to depend upon the proved, they lost excitement for stories and fairies and exaggerations. As their fiction depended less on the imagined so did their autobiography. They became almost two-dimensional. Firm and hopeless objects. The one thing about facts is they must be committed to memory. They are of no real use unless they can be called up to prove a point. There is a danger if a person's entire life is based on fact.

If everything must be remembered, what is left when it is forgotten?

Drury had listened by the old fires to travellers telling tales of the great island. He knew only some of it was true, but loved the pieces that had been invented. Sometimes the travellers listened as others told the stories of their own lives. Drury noticed these autobiographies were constructed with two materials. If a gap in the true sections of the story threatened to collapse it, the gap was filled with invention. Similarly, when the exaggeration seemed too far-fetched it was bolstered by truth. Drury saw that the best stories were not pure fantasy and not pure fact. One fell without the other.

The history of Nottingham is a story where the surface becomes more important than that which runs beneath it. Tigguacobaucc was overwhelmed by its big pretty younger sister. Over time people stopped living in caves altogether and surfaced to trade and laugh in the sunlight. Going underground was gradually forgotten, and with that practice, the undercurrents of autobiography were lost. The people of Nottingham have discarded their routine of reflection. They no longer give thought to what might have happened, only that which they have evidence for. They are not unusual in this but when life ceases beneath the surface of a place its people become shallow. In the absence of depth stories are flat and autobiographies are just stories. Buildings need hard and soft material.

Personal things. The story of one person is no more fact than fiction; it is both. But to see that this is a truth takes an open mind. It is uncertain if other stories exist, but this is enough to make them important. Historical fact and the fabulous, dreams and reality, Tigguacobaucc and Nottingham, journeys between the lines. If a person does not consider that essentials may go unseen then they will become confused; if Nottingham dismisses Tigguacobaucc it is only half a city. When people do not scratch the surface of their lives they have only the surface. Tigguacobaucc and Nottingham are interdependent; each needs its opposite, for where one is without the other there is no poetry. The story of a person can be lost entirely or can twist into many others.

A person with no story is a diseased person. As is a person with too many.

These are the things that Drury has seen and told me about. These are the lost things of Tigguacobaucc, but they are not the only things. One aspect of the ancient life of Nottingham has survived. The hereditary cannot be hidden because it does not care about remembrances or forgetfulness. Blood has no time for woes and happiness. Medical conditions have no concern for the vessels that hold them, they are parasitic proof that science can be vicious. Down through the centuries of history that have turned Nottingham into the greatest city in the world, a line of weak creatures have doggedly reproduced more of themselves. There has always been a hyperbilirubinæmic Ringmaster clinging to the spin of Canning Circus.

His job has decreased in importance as the caves have done. The Circus has vanished and become an undercurrent to life in Nottingham. The place that once stood for the understanding of personal stories is now as secondary to life in this city as Tigguacobaucc. Whiston is the last of the yellow-skinned, the end of a tradition. This is the case because he has no children so no-one will inherit his post. Many things are in his blood but many of them are diluted. His grip on the magic of Canning Circus is loose because the people of Nottingham need neither him nor the place where he was born.

Whiston does not even have the menial tasks of someone who cares for a magic place, because Canning Circus has not been recognised as magical for centuries. But in his blood is information on the tradition of his yellowed ancestors; he has been born to be the Ringmaster. Whiston is born to remind storytellers that other journeys may exist within the lines of one journey. He is genetically programmed to maintain a place where answers can be found, where The Rings cannot grapple. On Canning Circus the air will clear around stories and autobiographies to allow their tellers a view of all lines. Canning Circus is a haven of the unrecorded, the hidden links. Up there it is possible to know more than fact and in so doing become three-dimensional. Reflection on Canning Circus can allow anything to happen, and anything will.

Magic is the art of inventing the truth, but also of finding it.

Here is Whiston's tragedy. This is a man designed for a purpose but unable to carry it out. He can see the undercurrent of Canning Circus. When he stands at the window of the flat in which he was born, his eyes take in the surface. He feels the confusion of those who sit at the edge, he knows their fear. He watches the confident move in and out of pubs and shops, following their eager steps. In the speed of their gait he sees the urgency of life and its excitement. Whiston knows that Nottingham seems enough for these people. It is a city that has survived and grown more beautiful. People are happy here in a gallop through days. They are entertained, wined and loved. Around them is the ancient and the modern. Nottingham is a fast city where even the old have good reason to consider themselves young, for all of them move in a place many times older than their own bodies. There is terrible violence here but it never threatens to overwhelm the town. Nottingham has not lost its heart, though some of its inhabitants have lost theirs. Whiston understands that these people cannot feel the need to reflect on what may have happened because what does happen is distraction enough. Whiston watches Canning Circus just as any of us watch it. He knows the shops are filled with costumes and junkery. He saw what I saw: Dick Turpin, Bugs Bunny and an orange cow crossing the road a few years ago, being careful of the traffic. He knows that the people inside the costumes were having fun, making the most of an evening. He knows they meant themselves no harm. Whiston sees the inadvertency of fun.

By the skills that accompany his sickness he can see through the costume around the skin and through the skin into the heart and lungs. Though he does not speak the language of medicine, Whiston has a loose grip on magic. In his eyes these happy people are shadows of who they could be. They are attached to only half of life. Their light feet traipse across Canning Circus without stopping. They make no decisions. They are unconscious to magic.

And here is how The Rings began to grab Whiston by his weak throat. He has spent all his life looking onto Canning Circus. He stands at the window scratching his arms, being aware of other people's entropy. It is strange that in a place of costume people give no thought to things which may be disguised. When they remove the layer that covers their skin and stand naked, Whiston knows they believe they have become vulnerable, that nothing is left to hide. But a mirror cannot reflect unseen things. Nor can it replace that which is lost. Black Boy never found his heart by collecting mirrors, he only saw more images of an incomplete body. But Whiston has the blood of the Ringmaster, blood that tells him to look deeper. He knows that going underground into the arches and passageways of stories will reveal other stories. In the clinical terminology of his disease lies the ability to diagnose illness in others. From

Whiston's own weakness comes the tradition of giving strength to a place that gives strength.

But he cannot perform his task alone and he is alone. The Rings have set in as secure as the sandstone which forms Canning Circus. The Rings have him. They have grappled him to the ground in the place where he would once have been safe. In his concentration on the disjointed lives of all he sees, Whiston has become concentric. In his ability to watch the indecision of others he has become obsessed with decision. Whiston's mind is always made up.

His acute blood digs for the stories of the people of Nottingham because they do not dig themselves. He is a manic archæologist looking for a small glitter in the sand, a roll of dice, a story. He prepares The Circus in his thoughts for thoughts of others who never come. Whiston can do nothing for people who do not want him. Whiston watches the clock above Canning Terrace. Whiston has too much time on his hands. Canning Circus will not let him go.

The Rings hold him as they do all of us and his throat has not had the volume to be heard above the traffic and revellers. On some desperate nights he has called into the busy air, but even the keen ears of an orange demon could not hear him. Whiston has been alone in the epicentre of Canning Circus with the stories of thousands. In the flat where he outlived his mother and father, Whiston began to suffocate. He had neither air nor love. In those stiff rooms he folds himself into a fret. If Nottingham has grown strong enough to hide an entire city beneath it, then it has easily absorbed a sick curiosity from a long-forgotten tradition.

The people of Tigguacobaucc believed that the most fertile ground pro-duces most riches. In this logic they were not simple but at the same time not lost. They had logic but there was no argument and so they did not suffer confusion. Situations did not run in circles and The Rings could not exist without complexity. But Whiston sees the complex, festering in my stories.

My name is Tigguacobaucc but it is a name that does not suit me. It heralds from a time when people saw fairies as important as facts. The name implies a knowledge of caves, which I do have, and a knowledge of my own hidden places, which I do not have. I am unmapped. My autobiography has merely skirted the truth. Most of it has been invention. I never thought I would hear myself say this but I need some facts of my own, to bolster the weaknesses of my exaggerations. This is not to say that I am disappointed in the way I have told the stories of my friends; they at least seem satisfied. But I am not. These stories have a greater purpose than simply to entertain. They are meant to lead me towards my own story. According to Old Angel, in their invention I am to find truth. I am a librarian and my job is the storage of fact. But I have made the mistake of bringing work home and so have begun to depend on fact alone to give my life its structure. I have disregarded many things that once cemented me. My name is Tigguacobaucc. A replacement name in a city of two parts. Nottingham has welcomed me as it has welcomed you and I am safe here but confused. My mind is a conglomerate, a meeting of many others who do not understand the nature of The Rings any more than I do. The Rings are manifested differently in each of us, preying on points of weakness like a mantis, prying into us, setting us into a spin. My Rings are terrible; they have blanked me, blanketed me with the stories of others. If I tell each story, each layer that covers me, I will bare myself and remember. Sticks and stones. Sticks and stones may break my bones. My name is Tigguacobaucc but it is not my name. I want back the name I cannot remember, the name that can pull me from The Rings, the name that can never hurt me. There is a manifestation. I cannot help but repeat myself. You may have noticed before but I have only this minute become aware of it. Black Boy. Corner Pin. Hickling Laing. Drury. Rouse. Old Angel. Jalland. Whiston. Plumtre. A genuine mish-mash. They are the principal rocks. The fossil of my story is to be found curled in the sediment of theirs. Old Angel, you are the biggest devil of them all. It was your voice that raised my hopes, yet I have come this far and found so little of myself. I have committed to memory my whole life. I have ordered and stored for easy retrieval. I have classified my life and made it a library. I am a foolish creature. It should be obvious that danger lurks between the shelves of this approach. I have been taught that the great risk for the existence of libraries is that all the information is in one place, and if that place is destroyed or forgotten then so too is the information. This has happened to me. The Rings have caught me by the scruff of the neck and shaken me until my library—my life—lay in heaps on the floor. In those hundreds of documents which are all memories is my chronology. But I am caught in The Rings, because if I reorder them and reshelve them I run the risk of it happening again, of being struck twice by lightning. I have at least learnt that much. But what else? In these stories is the hard material of my life, which can be formed with the soft material from my often ethereal friends into the story of my life. There. There is something I now believe to be true. Before telling these stories I could not have said that fairies are fact, that the insubstantial can be strong. I would not have accepted myself as two-dimensional without a knowledge of magical things. In my organised happiness before The Rings took hold, my arrogance knew no bounds. Imaginary beings were things for children; they were entertainments. I could not have believed that they would enhance my life in the way that Jalland has made me richer. I was incapable of seeing that air and love are The Necessary. I walked unconscious across Canning Circus.

Over hundreds of years, Drury has watched the people of Tigguacobaucc throw off the past much as I threw away things I considered to be childish. They wanted the new. Recently returned travellers were treated like princes while they told of the latest discoveries on the great island, but as soon as their story was done the people watched for more travellers. In their urge to be thrilled and entertained the people of Tigguacobaucc failed to value that which had thrilled them in the past. These old stories did not know what to do with themselves. They floated into the sky but always kept The Circus in sight. Sometimes birds would accidentally catch on them and they would be flown thousands of miles to another continent. These stories would fall exhausted to the earth and be misunderstood by the people of strange countries. It was more common though for the stories to gather above The Circus and hang around. They could not lie down because each successive Ringmaster was sure to dispose of them in his preparations. So the stories gathered over The Circus for centuries.

It is true that most Ringmasters, even though they had no choice in the matter, were devoted to their work. But it must be remembered they were chosen because they had yellow skin from illness. The Ringmasters have always been the only people with the ability to see stories as objects in their own right. After all, it was the Ringmaster who reminded storytellers that things can exist that are not seen. These men could see the gathering stories but did not have the strength to clear them out of the sky. The storytellers did not believe that stories could exist without their voices. This is usual for storytellers. Most of them think they own their stories, and so do not see that what they have created is always more complex than they could imagine. All stories contain others between their lines.

Canning Circus, as The Circus is now known, has an invisible cloud of stories hanging over it. Whiston can see them of course and the disorder makes him feel more sick each day. I cannot see them but if I listen carefully I can hear them. They are the stories of one thousand years of Nottingham and Tigguacobaucc and they are tangled and complicated. They have nowhere to go and a Ringmaster who can do nothing to help them. He is too absorbed in the lost stories of living people to aid the trapped stories of the long dead.

Whiston will not live forever, though he might. This is Canning Circus. Anything happens here and anything does. Whiston has watched anything happen many times except the one happening he hopes for. Whiston is not unusual in his hope, for he hopes one fine day to be set free. He is the last Ringmaster but does not wish to spend the last years of his life being it. The tradition was weakened in his blood simply by being filtered through so many generations, so he could not have accepted his post with blind duty. This is compounded by the fact that no-one feels the need to use Canning Circus as it has been used in the ancient days, when Tigguacobaucc was more important than Nottingham. Whiston is a product of a one thousand year old line and of a modern city. It is natural for confusion to hold him in a grip that makes him gasp for air and love.

Shaped unlike a circle it is circular. Without a big top it is still a circus. I am almost too late to be its storyteller; imagination has already run riot about it, and most of that imagination is a restless shade of stories going nowhere. Canning Circus seems to be my last hope. There must be enough magic left in the old place. Whiston may find his life has not been useless. I think he and Drury should make plans while keeping an eye on that clock; Whiston is not looking too good. Canning Circus is the place to be. I've learnt that much.

chapter

the story of plumtre

T HE thousands of stories tangled in the sky over Canning Circus have sometimes been plucked from the cloud by fairies. They are homeless now, but all formerly sheltered in the lives of people that are long dead. Each is the story of a person or place and many have travelled long distances in the minds of travellers. These are stowaway stories, that once hid in the vehicular minds of the restless. For as long as language could be taken down, the stories found themselves bustled from their foreign lands and retold in Nottingham. They were thrown carelessly into a careless crowd.

When Plumtre was born he broke his mother's banks in her poor home. The father had left to find higher ground, where his fertile land could not be flooded by the waters of commitment. Plumtre was a tiny Tristanton, a trespasser on the furrows of his father's sex life. At the beginning it appeared that Plumtre would not move from the nothing his mother gave him. It was chance that Jalland heard the waterfall birth. It was chance that the story he tugged from Canning Circus was one to make Plumtre rich. Chance gave Plumtre a famous story. Chance brought lions into his garden.

On the first night of Plumtre's life Jalland fluttered into his room. He landed beside the little head and whispered a whole story into the fresh mind. The baby was born poverty-stricken, without a story, but when he woke his mind was rich. The story of Plumtre was only a matter of time. And as is common in a life of great purpose this time passed quickly. Plumtre grew up with little money but many values. His mother was proud of him but she did not understand why he would not eat meat. Plumtre could never fathom this either but he became a man on pulses and vegetables. Even when his voice deepened and hairs covered his arms he had strong beliefs on food. Plumtre also never drank wine, only water. He had not made these decisions; they were who he was.

Early in his life Plumtre realised he had an ability to interpret dreams and visions. He constantly amazed his mother by telling her the meanings of dreams she could not even remember. Plumtre's mother looked at the house she was forced to raise her son in and thought she had lost out. She decided that dreams were not for the likes of her, that someone who could barely afford vegetables could hardly afford to dream. But Plumtre brought light and magic into his mother's life. He showed that her dreams were rich places. He gave her another life and made her night inventions into truths. She worked hard to provide for them both, and never took holidays. She had thought that this was the way of her world, but Plumtre turned his mother into a great traveller when she went to sleep.

Plumtre has always been a lover of Nottingham, and when he was a young man he decided to work for the city. The first job he had was an insignificant post in The Council House, where he was responsible for checking and sending out bills for parking tickets. This was not rewarding work but Plumtre knew he had to start somewhere. During the day his brain performed menial and routine tasks, but at night he soared because he had Jalland as a friend. For his whole life Plumtre had been able to see and talk to fairies. Their stories held many messages, but Jalland could never repair the chip on his silver shoulder or set free the bee from his glittering hair. Plumtre was warned constantly that Nottingham would become a shadow of its ancient sister, Tigguacobaucc. Jalland told him time was running from the clock on Canning Terrace into the graves beneath it. He said that if Nottingham continued to misunderstand the imaginary then it might lose its imagination completely. The surface people of Nottingham never thought about what might run in the caves under them. They looked into the sky and saw no fairies or demons or stories. They had no expectation. They had almost lost their imagination so they could not catch the imaginary going about their work. Nottingham was losing grip on invention and so too on truth.

Plumtre heard all of this and swore to use his talent for seeing the purpose of dreams and visions to the good of the city. After he had worked with parking tickets for a year, his colleagues knew him quite well. In fact his ability to interpret dreams and quell the fears of those in his office had become well known. It was only a matter of time before word of his skill reached the top of his city. One fine day he was asked to visit immediately the Sheriff of Nottingham, who was in a terrible state.

The Sheriff was a good man. He was strict but admired by his employees and none of them had ever seen him so nervous or tense. The Sheriff could not recall what his dream had been about, only that it had disturbed him deeply. He rang round everyone he thought might help him, but the psychiatrists, preachers, astrologers and agony aunts could do nothing for him. They were unable to interpret a dream that could not be recalled. The Sheriff grew more and more impatient. He threw everyone out of his office and put his head in his hands. While it was there he remembered some gossip that was going round the council, that a young man in Parking Tickets was able to tell you about your dreams. The Sheriff decided that anything was worth a try and sent for Plumtre. When he arrived in the Sheriff's office Plumtre listened carefully to his boss. Plumtre asked for time and said he would come into work the next day with an answer. When he got home that night he spoke to Jalland as usual, but asked Jalland to tell him the dream that had been blown into the Sheriff's ear by one of his folk. He listened and then slept soundly.

The next day he washed and dressed vigorously before getting the bus to work. Plumtre went straight to the Sheriff's office for he was filled with confidence. The Sheriff looked up and sat back with his arms folded. Plumtre told him of the dream he could not recall and of its meaning. He said that it was a warning to the Sheriff that Nottingham was in danger of losing its magic because the people of the city either did not believe in the magical, or misunderstood it when they did. Plumtre said that the Sheriff had dreamt of Standard Hill, where Nottingham Castle perched. He reminded the Sheriff that Nottingham had been the furnace of the English Civil War and that in those days the city had great importance. Plumtre told the Sheriff that the city would be ignored, that it would become dulled—as its people had become—to magic. Sherwood Forest, once a great Royal Hunting Forest, would continue to shrink and fade. Eventually Major Oak, a symbol of the huge history of Nottingham, would be dead. The city would fall under the shadow of many others and be forgotten. Plumtre said that Nottingham could still be saved. It was a city full of imaginary beings; even God had decided to live there and had fallen in love. But if they were ignored they too would grow weak, and Nottingham's strength had always drawn from the magical. It was a city of myth and legend where anything could happen. Nottingham must celebrate its inventions and see them as truths. This gave the Sheriff an idea. He smiled for the first time in two days and rewarded Plumtre's conviction and wisdom with a promotion. Plumtre moved from Parking Tickets to Deputy Head of Leisure. This irked some very irksome people.

Just as Drury feels misrepresented, the Sheriff misunderstood the interpretation of the warning given to him by Jalland's folk. His idea was well-meaning but mistaken. The Sheriff decided to celebrate Nottingham's myths. He found the money in his budget to erect a massive statue of Robin Hood in the middle of Old Market Square, and invited dignitaries from other cities as well as all the people of Nottingham to its unveiling. The huge lake of concrete was covered with excited bodies, for though Nottingham is a big city it is still communal. Many thousands stared eagerly at the towering drape but did not gasp when it was pulled away. In their hearts and lungs they had wanted the magical, they needed signs and wonders. They saw a slab of concrete.

The Sheriff tried to celebrate Nottingham by building another substantial image instead of welcoming the insubstantial, the imaginary. He did not realise that Nottingham is special due to its magic. The unveiling was a failure because the people were not moved or improved by simply an image of someone they believed to be dead, if they even believed the legend of Robin Hood in the first place. Nottingham still did not know that Robin Hood was giving comfort and entertainment to an angry man beneath their feet.

The Sheriff of Nottingham tried to explain why he had erected the statue in Old Market Square. He wrote to the Nottingham Evening Post. In his letter he said that he was trying to show the people the wonders of their history. It did not cross his mind that he had unveiled an invention of Robin instead of a truth. Though he meant well, his mind still could not see that history is a random floating space. It is well known that the past is a lost place. It is well known that historians can sift through it for facts. It is not well known that anyone can stumble upon facts if they believe in the imagination, that they might trip over Robin Hood if only they expected to.

Jalland decided to give the Sheriff a second chance, a second dream. And as Jalland would say, when dreams lose their harmony they become nightmares. Their concord turns to discord, and William Shakespeare knows that without fairies the concord to such a discord cannot be found. The Sheriff's second dream made him call in all his experts again, and again they could not interpret it. But Plumtre had his ears to the air, and after he had spoken with Jalland he told the Sheriff his dream and the meaning of it.

The Sheriff dreamt he was walking in Sherwood Forest. For much of his walk the light threw itself through the trees playfully. He was enjoying himself. The responsibilities of his position were left in the hustle of the city and he had time to reap what he had sown: a town of wealth and beauty. The Sheriff patted himself on the back for his services to Nottingham. He did not have a proclivity to indulge in self-congratulation but he was still proud of how he carried out his duties. In the dream he was shown a normally hidden side to himself. He guzzled down his achievements and found they tasted good. The trees of Sherwood Forest looked beautiful in the sunlight and he walked on. The Sheriff found himself face-to-face with Major Oak and suddenly a change ran over his body like sweat. A red axe appeared in his hand and a massive anger swept from deep within him. He began to hack at the bark of the ancient tree and did not stop until it was a stump. Major Oak was the symbol of Nottingham and the Sheriff himself had felled it. As soon as the tree lay in twigs the Sheriff found himself turned into a rat. In his dream the fairies turned him into a lowly creature without pride or accomplishment. He was forced to spend the rest of his life watching helplessly as Nottingham withered.

These are the things that the Sheriff heard from Plumtre's lips, and he was afraid. The Sheriff promised to accept that the unseen could be as true as the seen. He threw a great party in The Council House to pronounce his decision, but he became carried away by the pomp of his robes and chain. He loved the attention heaped on him by the specially invited guests who were all powerful and learned people in the city. In his good humour and absorption he forgot entirely the reason for the party. This did not go unnoticed by Jalland who was on a windowsill, waiting to flit into the ballroom and be seen when the Sheriff declared him to exist. But without the words that would cause people to believe, Jalland remained invisible to all in the room except Plumtre.

Suddenly, amidst the din of dinner the Sheriff of Nottingham screamed for silence. A quietness fell over the crowd like gossamer because all their eyes were transfixed to one of the ballroom's wide walls. Jalland was writing on the wall, but all the Sheriff could see were words forming. Words written in a strange language. Immediately, the Sheriff grabbed his experts and pulled them away from the waists of their women. In the room were handwriting and linguistics professors from Nottingham University. The Sheriff pleaded with the linguists to translate the writing on the wall, but it was beyond them. They said it was like nothing they had seen before. The handwriting experts looked closely at the script and suggested that by its flair and curl it was almost inhuman. None of them could translate the strange message. But in the confused rumpus Jalland had whispered the translation into Plumtre's ear.

Plumtre stood up on a table and asked for quiet. He said that the message was short and to the point. It was written in the language of the fairies and contained a warning from them. If the people of Nottingham continued to repress their imaginations then their city would become second-rate. The people had wanted signs and wonders and now here was one, written in a strange script on the wall. Plumtre said if this was not evidence enough then the City of Nottingham was sure to fall under the shadows of cities more ugly and less magical.

The Sheriff listened to Plumtre and was once again struck by the wisdom and skill of this extraordinary young man. He climbed onto the table next to Plumtre and said two things: that all the people of Nottingham should open their minds and understand the magic that pulsed in their city; that from the following day, Plumtre was promoted to the post of Deputy Sheriff of Nottingham. The irksome members of the council were irked even further by both of these things. They decided to conspire against the young man who had risen rough-shod through their ranks.

And the size of things is what youth is all about.

These were unremarkable men and women who had worked in the council for most of their lives. Their promotions had moved at the speed of a glacier. They had never seen someone promoted like rapids. These are the jealous, the freezing, and they hated a youth whose career ran with such energy. They re-fused to see themselves as frozen between mountains of disbelief. They did not look into the wide magical eyes of Plumtre and catch his twinkling freedom. Instead these people set a watch on Plumtre's house.

It was common knowledge that Plumtre had bought a grand house in The Park, the red brick virtuoso outskirt to Nottingham Castle. It was also known that he had one of the most desirable properties in that area of desirable prop-erties. This was due to the garden that swept down from the house. In this garden is a group of caves containing ornamentation and carvings unsurpassed anywhere else in Nottingham. The house originally belonged to a wealthy busi-nessman and Alderman of the city, Herbert, who had made his fortune in the Lace Market. The house stands on The Ropewalk, a tightrope street overhanging The Park Estate, and the garden runs down over terraces into Park Valley.

Beneath the terraces of his garden, Alderman Herbert had a series of caves cut. The work probably took place around 1840 and their strange extravagance mean they are Victorian follies, pointless wonders. There are three caves in the series. The first is entered by a magnificent staircase hewn from the sandstone. This is Columns Cave, a large room supported by eighteen pillars. The lowest cave is called the Herbarium Cave. It has a central font and animals in bas-relief on the walls and supporting columns. The images combine to make this a cave of the grotesque. In between these two caves is the most remarkable cave in Nottingham, for it contains life size carvings of six lions. The lions have been made directly from the walls and are thought destined never to move. But such a point of view is symptomatic of Nottingham's disbelief.

This was the final malady.

Plumtre's enemies watched his house day and night. They hoped to discover an aspect of his life that would discredit him, that they could use to destroy him. They also followed him wherever he went in Nottingham but could find nothing damaging. Plumtre was a good man. Some of them worked in the accounts department of the council and so had access to many of Plumtre's private papers. But they could find no twisted figures or unpaid debts. Plumtre lived a clean life. He was a man of wisdom, but the root of that wisdom would prove dangerous.

In all the times he had interpreted dreams for the Sheriff he had not given away the source of his ability. Plumtre had told the Sheriff many times that his dreams were warnings from imaginary beings, but he had not decided the best way to tell the Sheriff that he had personal contact with those same beings. Consequently, the Sheriff believed he had an extraordinary young man as his deputy, but not one who actually talked to fairies. Plumtre's enemies could not believe their luck when one night they followed him out to Sherwood Forest.

Jalland had invited Plumtre to a fairy ball deep amongst the trees. This was no ordinary ball. It was one with a sad purpose. The councillors drove at a discreet distance behind Plumtre's car. Plumtre stopped at the gates to the forest and the councillors drove past so as not to arouse suspicion. They pulled up round the next corner and ran quickly back to the gates. They climbed over them and made for a whooping sound in the darkness. They peered from behind some trees and could not believe what they saw, or rather they could only see what they believed.

There were many fairies darkening the grass into rings with their dance. Plumtre jiggled and drank from a specially made, and therefore giant bowl of nectar. The fairies downed their sweet sorrow from tiny flowers. All around Plumtre's head were fairies spinning in moonlight that dripped from the leaves of Sherwood as only light can drip. The councillors saw that Plumtre was dancing around the millennial trunk of Major Oak. The councillors only saw what they believed, what they expected. For them there were no fairies, no small music, no dripping moonlight. They watched their Deputy Sheriff moving alone under the symbol of Nottingham, lifting nothing to his lips, chattering and laughing loudly. They considered him mad.

Then Plumtre stopped dancing and sat in the moss. The councillors moved as close as they dared to listen, because Plumtre appeared to be talking to himself. Jalland and the other fairies explained to Plumtre that Major Oak was tired. The huge tree had enjoyed its life but now wanted nothing more than to be allowed to die. The fairies said that Major Oak should no longer be forced to live. For the sake of tourism, the tree was kept alive. Its ancient branches were supported by planks of wood and if a wound opened in the bark it was filled with chemicals. This tree wanted to die. The fairies said they understood the importance of Major Oak to the health of Nottingham, but if the people of the city could see and accept the imaginary they would no longer be dependent on physical links with their past. There were many beings, not least Robin Hood, who desperately wanted to be welcomed back to Nottingham as heroes. This ball was to celebrate the life of Major Oak but also to lay him to rest. Plumtre told the fairies that he knew the people of Nottingham's quixotic feelings towards the tree. He said that if he was given enough time he might be able to explain the tree's own feelings. Plumtre said it was his opinion that Major Oak should have been allowed to die, that the image of Nottingham should be cut down.

These last words were the only ones heard by Plumtre's enemies. They raced back to their car with hearts crammed with wicked joy. They would tell the Sheriff in the morning that not only did his Deputy dance like a madman in Sherwood, but also that he was hatching plans to destroy the gnarled symbol of their city. And the jealous councillors were cunning as well as envious. They thought of a plan which they were sure would give Plumtre no way out. He would be stuck.

The next day the councillors burst into the Sheriff's office. He looked up and saw that they all wore serious smiles. They told him everything they had seen that night. The Sheriff was angry, but not particularly with Plumtre. His anger came from embarrassment that he could have appointed a madman so high into his administration. He agreed with the councillors that Plumtre's sanity should be tested; it would not look good for his judgment of character if Plumtre was simply sacked for dancing with fairies. He did not understand why Plumtre had warned him through the interpretation of his dreams that Major Oak was in danger, while at the same time plotting to let the tree die. The Sheriff could not understand because he had never truly believed. He still gripped the idea that he was responsible for the success of Nottingham himself. The Sheriff was unable to see that the life of Major Oak had become one of eternal sadness.

He listened as the councillors relayed their plan. In its checkmate they had made a long leap of the imagination. Plumtre lived in a famous house with an even more famous garden. Under his garden, six stone lions grew from the wall of the cave that held them captive. The councillors realised that if Plumtre really did believe in the imaginary then these sandstone lions might come to life in his presence; inventions may become truths. The lions, imagined and carved, were harmless to someone who did not believe they could pounce. To Plumtre they could be fatal. He would be hunted down by his imagination. The councillors told the Sheriff to lock Plumtre in the lion's cave overnight. And here was what they thought to be their masterstroke. If Plumtre was not mad his body would be gnashed. If he survived the night then he was mad and unfit to hold public office. Either way, Plumtre would be finished. When he arrived for work, the Sheriff ordered him to make a choice. He was to have the courage of his convictions or resign on grounds of mental health. The Sheriff knew already what Plumtre's answer would be.

That night he was escorted back to his home in The Park and locked in the cave of lions. The Sheriff took the key and went home. He was exhausted but could not sleep. He was not an evil man and had genuinely tried to improve life for the people of Nottingham. The Sheriff thought over all the times that Plumtre had interpreted his dreams and visions. He lay in bed with his hands behind his head and began to piece together the words of this wise young man. He tossed over and over the messages his dreams had given him through Plumtre. He thought of Major Oak and the writing on the wall. His closed mind under-went a kind of conversion. The Sheriff saw that his people's belief in magic had for centuries been selfish. He thought of God and of the people of Nottingham imagining a being to serve their own weaknesses. He realised that imaginary beings might have their own weaknesses, their own needs. He felt his people hurling themselves at an imaginary being only in times of crisis, giving no thought to the cares of imaginary beings. His skin prickled with the ugliness and shallow nature of their spirits. In his heart the Sheriff knew that Plumtre was not mad, but merely a bottle floating on a precarious sea with a desperate message from the fairies.

And Drury saw the Sheriff's thoughts and saw that they were good.

The Sheriff knew that Plumtre was wise and gentle. He stared into the darkness of his bedroom right through the jealousy of his councillors. But he thought that his realisation had come too late, for if Plumtre was not mad, then by morning his body would be in bloody pieces.

The Sheriff got out of bed early and dressed through bagged eyes. He walked through his city, up Derby Road and across Canning Circus into The Park to Plumtre's house. He unlocked the door and descended the wide sandstone staircase into the lion's cave. He made himself call out Plumtre's name, expecting no answer. But from the cold came Plumtre's bright voice. At least one of them had enjoyed a good night's sleep. The Sheriff walked further into the cave and there he saw an amazing sight. Plumtre sat amongst the lions with a silver fairy flitting around his head, and around the mouths of the lions were silver muzzles, glinting in the dim light.

The Sheriff was overjoyed and later that day sacked the wicked councillors. He rewarded Plumtre for his bravery with great wealth and a key to the City of Nottingham.

It has not been easy for the Sheriff. He has even been accused of madness himself, but he has done his best. The authorities over Nottingham are acceptable. They do not stand between us and life. They have never sealed the favourite entrances to Tigguacobaucc. They are good listeners. Because of Plumtre and the Sheriff we have been able to go underground for these stories. But there are as many stories hanging over Nottingham as there are running beneath it. We at least know the place of conclusion and of beginning. It was chance that brought Plumtre and his story together. I am hopeful. Canning Circus waits to become a meeting place once more.

It was Jalland who protected Plumtre from the beasts. It was Jalland all along. Even Drury admits that this story is an echo of an earlier one. An invention and a truth. The Book of Daniel. The Story of Plumtre. This is one old story plucked from the cloud above Canning Circus and found a rich home. Drury remembers as if it was only yesterday. A fairy's writing on the wall being mistaken for his own. I have warned you of the lions in Plumtre's garden many times, but you need only fear them if you believe the imagined can come to life. I for one must watch my step.

chapter **10** the rings

a circle and a revelation

FOLLOW me over. The Rings are rearing their rhythm. Give me another drink; I am stuck with loving. You have held close to my words and learnt new hiding places, silent places for thoughts to run, dark places for bodies to slide against other bodies. Here, torn from buff Sherwood sandstone, are great passages and arching rooms held by wide pillars. For hundreds of metres these caves pass under the city, and we choose to follow them. They have become galleries for our work, shelters for our weaknesses, chambers in which to rejoice and remember. And sitting before me are my Rings, the people whose stories have circled my own. My friends, you devils.

I am a librarian and I have shelved for easy retrieval all that has happened to me. I watched myself from childhood carefully, not wishing to misplace a single minute of this life. I felt I should be rewarded for my self-control, praised for my powers of organisation. I was born with a librarian's brain so I became one. Caves and libraries are the holy rooms for my spirit. I remember as a child spending hours finding places in which to breathe the unpopular air of corners. Habits do not die and I have made a career from pungence. Air and love. I've always searched for words that could bring both down on my head; I am not afraid of making wishes. I am an improviser. I make do with what I've got at any moment, and I have never felt both air and love. Always one without the other. Never The Necessary. In front of me my friends sit in the sand. It is entwined in their stories that my own story hides, twirled beyond recognition. Old Angel told me to repeat everything I knew of these stories and I have done. Old Angel told me that this process might release my story from its bindings. And it almost has done so. I feel neglect because I've left myself to last. Who am I? A genuine mish-mash.

The Rings will be manifested differently in each person, though they will grip each as tightly as the next. They are depression, entrapment, work, a great loss. The Rings bore under the skin and carry out damage to the tenderness that lies beneath it. They do not understand the language of medicine and leave the body raw when they have done their circular business. Any situation that runs in circles can become The Rings. They are the *departments* of a city strung out over the airwaves. They are even the vast growth of a city relentlessly over its roots, destroying the forest that once gave it safety. The Rings make the safe unsafe, the clean unclean, the shelved a fallen mountain of confused papers. And here is my own dispersal. Each fluttered sheet is the information of my life. When my library collapsed I could not reshelve the mess. What happens if everything is committed to memory and an accident occurs? Memory lies in a white jumble.

I do believe that as far as possible we must take responsibility for what strikes us. I know that some will gain a higher quality of life simply by being born nearer the clouds. The north is steeper than the south. For the rest it is uncommon that chance will play an active role; luck is not a friend to most. They must quest within and without. If these people were professional historians they might wind down their lives sifting for the definite. In an average life it is reasonable to have some gold too big for the holes in it. There will be nuggets of happiness wherever the sieve hits the sand. But this approach is not sure enough for a crisis. I am called Tigguacobaucc but my name requires a lot of air around it, and the purpose of these stories is to clear air, to allow clean stuff through the tubes. I feel the verge of awakening, and where discoveries are falling over themselves to run The Rings from my blood.

Friends can be entertaining jailors. It is well known that you choose them and not your family. These are the people that prove life. They stare straight into the face and recognise you. They touch and sometimes love, they utter words in your direction. But The Rings have grabbed me where I am strongest, using my talents against me. I am capable of two things only: being a teller of stories; ordering libraries. The Rings misuse need, twist wishes. Confusion can be very convincing.

There is Black Boy. When he was younger he lost his heart. This would cause anyone to become interested in themselves. Narcissism was Black Boy's hobby and so began his collection of mirrors. But in them he only saw his broken-hearted remnants. Even a view of swans parading the Trent could not fill his empty chest. The Rings haunted his need for a replacement. They spun him in his desire for the animate, teasing girls from their clothes, giving him pleasure in seeing himself gilt-edged. But The Rings did not understand the language of medicine and so were no match for it. They had forgotten Black Boy's skill with his hands; they were found out by my books, left standing under the wisdom of an orange demon. Black Boy ran circles around The Rings. He moved towards the inanimate faster than they could push him into a love of girls or of himself. In his living room he constructed a heart. In his new heart he found faith in trees.

Black Boy found old gold.

Corner Pin has managed to stay still for all these stories. For someone so fast in his sadness this is remarkable. He has been hurt more than any of us. Corner Pin once mistook his father for a Norwegian, and this was only the second of many maladies. In his childhood there were two figures, God and the pain in his legs. His father invented an image of the first, and the second increased into a truth. The Rings took Corner Pin in their arms and pretended to cradle him. He curled into a sprint and heard nothing except his own thoughts. He shut the world out and screwed his face into a tight state. Within these redrawn borders the country that lay behind them became unrecognisable. I thought Corner Pin had let his common sense fall into one of the gutters he ran past, but he did what seemed impossible. He forced his voice that had been trapped by The Rings out between his teeth. Many things took the opportunity to run for it. Corner Pin screamed for help. He is yet to slow down but at least he is running in the right direction.

Corner Pin, I feel the pact of your sadness like a brother.

Hickling Laing is close to me because he began in Nottingham but left for a while, and he returned to become stuck with loving this one. Even at the beginning of this night of stories, I felt that my story could be told through his. A story of two parts. An invention and a truth. Hickling Laing entered my life at a crucial point. I remember. I recall where I first met him. Two of my friends have come to my library for help concerning the human body. Black Boy wanted the blueprint for a heart. Hickling Laing needed to prove our bodies are not miracles, just physics and chemistry. They both came at me like sharks, but not in the same library. I have been in Birmingham and fallen in love there.

Hickling Laing was born with disbelief in his eyes. They are oil black and he has used them well, but not only to convert the Christian. A red chair was his university, his laboratory. Between its high arms he read books and concocted reactions. And the truth for which he scanned stories suffered great stress under those black eyes. He could only be moved, taught, by exceptional books. They needed strong bindings and tight words to withstand the intense glare while he read them. Over time, many found themselves cast to the floor like bad seed, but others, the minority, grew in the environment Hickling Laing provided for them. These books were rarely read by someone who could give the attention that Hickling Laing shone into them. Like libraries, they will respond to palpation. It requires only the electricity running from the fingers of a sensitive reader to restart the phloem that was once their constitution. Books are the afterlife of trees.

Hickling Laing, I know you have not wasted your time.

When you spent one whole day talking to Drury you could not believe what you saw. But you could believe what you were hearing. You had devoted your whole life to proclaiming that God did not exist and in some ways you were right. You told people they worshipped something that did not want their worship, believed God could perform acts he could not perform. They accepted the words of a man who had merely been brave, and used his words to stand in judgment over others. They had listened to inventions and believed them to be truths. You pointed your fingers at all of this and an imaginary friend became your proof. You were not a madman. When you called for a companion Drury answered your safe prayer.

Drury, I feel your omnipresent eyes on the back of my neck like a lover.

Tap. Tap. Tap. Rouse is still in his shadows under the shadow of Ann, sitting at the sand-face of his labyrinth. Her sweet voice left him but his hero did not. His is a story of arrows and song and it has shown me much. Digging.

Rouse, you have given us a gallery for these stories; dig on old man, I am always glad to see your back working against the rock.

Old Angel, your words have suggested that I should use words to rid me of The Rings. Your voice has spawned my own voice. I can see it has been difficult for you to leave me and return to me. Do not be afraid of vibrations. Plumtre has secured a future for our caves. The Sheriff of Nottingham will not cover us in concrete. He believes in us. Old Angel, you enjoy listening and I enjoy talking; we are made for each other. I am used to your little habits, and in them I can see a revelation. Your habits are becoming my habits. Your philosophy on flowers fills my nose with its perfume.

Old Angel, your words calm me like the words of a father.

Jalland. Jalland. Jalland. You are looking well. I would apologise for being addictive but you are an imaginary being; you know I am only being human. You dance for your own enjoyment but also for the benefit of us, your friends. You dance every night all over Nottingham and in the morning ordinary people wake to find rings on their lawns. These circles of dark green grass are where you have danced on the spot. Of course, it is not only you Jalland who dances, there are many fairies who come to the aid of the big people during the night, who come to watch over them. I have it from Jalland's own tiny mouth that fairy dances once took place over all of England. His mouth has also said that fairies now only dance in Nottingham. Nowhere else has the magic to sustain them. What city is this? Nottingham. Why is it famous? For many reasons. What does it hide? Only fairies darkening the grass.

Jalland, I am a drug that means you no harm. A drug that loves you.

Whiston is on the surface preparing Canning Circus. In this work he is escaping The Rings himself. In Whiston's story The Rings gripped him in the absence of a story. They trapped him in a place full of stories yet held him from forging his own. But in their cruelty is their weakness. The Rings fear stories. I have overwhelmed the emptiness of my life with the rich words of others, and between those words I can see myself. Canning Circus waits to home the lost hanging above it, stories from under and over Nottingham. Imagination has run riot and even Jalland would admit that this is not good for the health.

Plumtre, what an amazing life you have had. Though it was not your own you made it so. You are one of the few whom luck befriended. I am proud to know you, though I will always wait for Jalland before visiting your garden.

Plumtre, you showed me that someone with no story can obtain one.

One thousand years ago in Tigguacobaucc a young man decided to become a traveller. For many years he had watched his mother perform delicate tasks and hung onto his father's hairy back in the hunt. He lived with the mother and the father in a large cave. He was not an only child for he had a younger brother and the forest was a wide garden. These were mysterious times and the two boys had brilliant imaginations. The first thing they believed in was a monster that roamed the trees and glinted its long teeth. They never saw it but counted this a success. With two friends they made a secret club to fight the monster. They would hunt it as their fathers hunted less dangerous creatures, racing through the under and over growth. That they never caught the imaginary proved to them its existence. Dreams are wily beasts.

Magic is the art of inventing the truth, but also of not finding it.

The four children grew beneath the trees and were happy. They had a traditional upbringing and so attended the reflection period each evening at The Circus. Up on the high rock they heard many stories. Most were the stories of people's lives, and though these people did not have significant dreams they were dreamers nonetheless. Their lives were rich with understanding for they spent a quiet time each day reflecting, not only on what had happened but on what might have happened. This practice brought understanding on their heads like rain.

At any moment we consider our friends permanent, but this is an uncommon thing. The four children thought they would run under the trees forever, but the two brothers were thrown from one another. Their two friends fell in love because they wanted familiar skin, but even in places of understanding there are rules and the brother and sister suffered epic deaths. The right to love and the right to find air were withheld. This is a common thing.

The story goes that the two brothers had been ignorant for years of the true relationship between their parents. The father was well known in the community for his astonishing talent to tell stories. He believed firmly in the place of The Circus in the lives of the people of Tigguacobaucc. Hundreds of times he told a hooked audience that Tigguacobaucc was the finest place to live, and that its people should never take for granted their place of caves and stories deep within the forest. The two brothers listened, but as they grew older a contradiction became clear to them. The father would tell his audience that it was essential to spend time with their children, to become part of their stories, but at home the father ignored his two sons. Their hearts and lungs were still severely shocked when he left. He had taught them to admire him.

The brothers were close but very different and they had opposite reactions to the loss of their father. Either way, even in that long ago land, The Rings caught their unbalance. Both began to run. The younger brother had, for as long as he had nerves, felt pain in his legs. This pain was training him to spend a fast life. He was primed to run aimlessly when his father made the home into a place of acute memory. The younger brother, though, ran even faster inside his heart than his legs could carry him. He investigated himself at great speed. Here The Rings exploited him for he gave no time to reflection and was lost. The elder brother ran away. As one home was destroyed he decided to create his own. His form of love was no more welcome at home than was the love of his childhood friends. The elder brother became a traveller.

He had sat on many evenings to the sound of stories from men who had walked everywhere. These tales said that Tigguacobaucc was in the centre of a massive island, and the elder brother thought he would investigate outside of himself. So both brothers ran, but in different directions. The younger brother found everything that was himself became a drug. The elder brother became addicted to everything that was not himself. The younger brother could recall only deep personal aspects. The elder brother gradually forgot the things that had made him. He lost himself in the stories of others and mislaid his own story. And it looked for a while as though the brothers would remain in these states for the rest of their lives. From their father they had each inherited habits. The younger brother ran into his own heart when life became difficult. The elder brother loved stories.

And it was stories that returned both him and his father to Tigguacobaucc. There was not enough magic away from the caves to sustain them. They had no air. But on their travels they had found love. The father had grown deeper in love with a woman beside the sea. The elder brother collapsed over his heels at the sight of a beautiful imaginary being. Both felt pulled back to The Circus.

When he returned, the elder brother could not recognise anyone. He had expected to find his birthplace unchanged, but the borders had been reworked. The past had become a different country. He was unable to see his brother's face when he stared into it. And he had grown unrecognisable to his brother. Neither could see past the changes to the familiar. They were strangers.

One thousand years ago this story has no ending. It had not happened before and so could not be a parable. It was unable to warn the brothers before their lives followed its direction, and powerless to help them when they had. But it is a risk for The Rings to trap people in repetition. With the correct mixture of friends, the lines of their stories may leave an opening where a lost story can be seen clearly in the tangle.

Black Boy. Corner Pin. Hickling Laing. Drury. Rouse. Old Angel. Jalland. Whiston. Plumtre. What have you got to say for yourselves? The Rings. A great loss and the repeat of it. In the angles made by your stories I can see myself; you are all just right for me. You have shown me that Nottingham is a place where anything can happen and anything does. Magic and the art of it. I have an ending from a story with no ending. I can feel air on my face and love on my shoulder in the random space left by someone one thousand years ago. My name is not Tigguacobaucc.

Old Angel: *Son. I'm sorry I left you for the ocean.*
Corner Pin: *Stay with me. My sadness is yours, brother.*
Drury: *Hello Car. I love you.*

You devils. I cannot be sure of what might have happened. I only know that in Nottingham more will be given than is taken away. This is the greatest city in the world. Here lies The Necessary. Home and stories running riot. My city could yet be the beginning of a new belief. I have come full circle, but there are many more whose stories hang over their city. It is time to throw fear at The Rings. Canning Circus, somewhere found for the lost. Come on, let's get some wind into the lungs.